The PROSPECT *of* MIRACLES

Also by Cyrus Mistry

FICTION

Chronicle of a Corpse Bearer
The Radiance of Ashes
Passion Flower: Seven Stories of Derangement

PLAYS

Doongaji House
The Legacy of Rage

{232}

The
PROSPECT
of MIRACLES

A NOVEL

CYRUS MISTRY

ALEPH

ALEPH BOOK COMPANY
An independent publishing firm
promoted by **Rupa Publications India**

First published in India in 2019
by Aleph Book Company
7/16 Ansari Road, Daryaganj
New Delhi 110 002

Copyright © Cyrus Mistry 2019

All rights reserved.

The author has asserted his moral rights.

This is a work of fiction. Names, characters, places and incidents are either the product of the author's imagination or are used fictitiously and any resemblance to any actual persons, living or dead, events or locales is entirely coincidental.

No part of this publication may be reproduced, transmitted, or stored in a retrieval system, in any form or by any means, without permission in writing from Aleph Book Company.

ISBN: 978-93-88292-99-3

1 3 5 7 9 10 8 6 4 2

For sale in the Indian subcontinent only.

Printed at Parksons Graphics Pvt. Ltd, Mumbai

This book is sold subject to the condition that it shall not, by way of trade or otherwise, be lent, resold, hired out, or otherwise circulated without the publisher's prior consent in any form of binding or cover other than that in which it is published.

*In memory of my late father, Behram
as also for
dear Mummy, Jill and Rushad*

I

DEATH OF A PASTOR

1

I sat on a hard plastic chair in a large, air-conditioned room.

Behind me, more rows of chairs; the hall was fast filling up with parishioners.

In deference to my special status, three chairs were reserved for me in the first row; even though I was all alone.

In the aisle to my right on a low steel pallet squatted the reason for this special status: my husband's coffin: he lay there in it, supine, lifeless, palms folded at the chest with a rosary entwined in his fingers as though engrossed in prayer.

A thin, voluble man took the podium. He had travelled all the way from Mattancherry to deliver a eulogy for the Pastor, my late husband.

∽

'…Oh pardon me please, allow me to rephrase: not mourn, dear friends—we will all miss him very much, undoubtedly we will continue to—but we, at the Mission of the Holy Spirit, do not mourn a brother who completes his term of earthly travails and flies into the loving embrace of Lord Jesus. Rather, we celebrate his release.

'So to those of you who feel sad, crestfallen or indeed dismayed, and especially to his lifelong partner, sister Agnes, I will say this: remember all the good times we shared with Pastor Philipose while he stood in our midst, encouraging us, enlivening our gloomiest moments with hope and love and an understanding born of wisdom; the same wisdom he shared with us every Sunday in church, and in recent times from this very podium…. You will recall what a wonderful preacher he was, Pastor Pius Philipose, how unforgettably his words touched all our lives….'

At this point, I stopped listening. My mind wandered back to my husband's bedside, two nights ago…. The vigil had been long and tiring, but at last, I felt the end was near: a moment ago when I touched his arm, then forehead and neck, his body seemed unnaturally cold; the icy shock of that sensation travelled to my heart at the speed of light, and chilled it.

∽

It was half past two in the morning. The night was warm, sticky, and unusually still. Cicadas, crickets, midges, gnats, creatures of the night, even the occasional soothing breezes, all fully sentient: aware, and overwhelmed by his passing. I felt his ice-cold arm once again. No doubt about it: the Pastor was truly dead and gone.

I lit a candle at his bedside.

We have a custom never to leave a dead body unattended. And I was longing to catch some sleep before morning….

There was only one way: Pauly. He'd be willing to keep vigil for the Pastor if I asked him.

Pauly is the sacristan at St Thomas Church next door, the one we owed allegiance to through all my childhood and youth. I know Pauly is always up by 3 a.m.

I wore my sandals and stepped out into the night. There was a nip in the air.

Presently, I was walking through a vast deserted churchyard and up the steps of a white confection-like structure whose ornate columns, cupolas and central spire glowed in the star-speckled night.

The heavy mahogany doors were shut, but one panel slightly ajar.

I shoved, and it gave with a creak. In the vast darkness inside, only a single dim bulb glowed at the far end of the nave. Pauly stood there, a short man, practically bald but with a dense beard of curls, polishing a silver candlestick.

'Kochamma!' he called in a loud whisper. 'Is Pastor better…?'

I shook my head.

'Pastor's gone….'

'Aah! I'm coming. Just give me five minutes to lock up.'

A few minutes later there he was, seated reverentially at the foot of the Pastor's bed; and I moved to my own smaller bedroom across the passage to try and get some rest.

But my breathing remained irregular; my heart fluttered just a bit as though still unconvinced this wasn't another cruel trick he was playing on me.

Towards morning I actually managed to doze off; then opened my eyes to see the Pastor silently padding into my room. He bent close over me, snarling, in his renowned, pulpit-ready stentorian:

'Did you think it would be so easy to get rid of me, woman? Ye of little faith, remember ye not how Lazarus rose even four days after death had seized his body? And from mine, I assure you, you won't detect the slightest whiff of putrefaction. Can you? Do you? Smell me, smell me!'

He brought his warty, furrowed face close to mine and touched it with the icy tip of his nose…. I woke up in a fit of shivering. A stench of stale cheese lingered in the room, even after I had shot up in bed realizing I had been dreaming.

☙

'As Archdeacon of the Governing Council,' a voice droned on, 'it gives me great pleasure to make an important announcement: we have decided to bring out a small volume of Pastor Pius Philipose's finest sermons....'

Not so long ago, the Pastor conducted his Sunday services at an austere Lutheran prayer-house. No stained glass, no ornamental crosses, no antique wooden pews; only a bare simplicity that was inspiring. But it was a wooden structure, alas. In the state-wide disturbances of four years ago, it was doused in kerosene one night and set afire by rioters. Many of the parishioners and, indeed, the Pastor himself, never quite recovered from the shock of that outrageous act of arson. A handful of goons were arrested by the police, but they are all out on bail.

Ever since, the diocese books this reception hall for Sunday services; but it's a commercial centre, also hired out for weddings, first communions, business conventions and election rallies. The restoration of the former Worship Centre is still not complete.

'I'm sure all of you would like your own copy when it's out. We aim to make it available in four to five weeks at most. I have the printer's assurance on that. That'll be something to look forward to, I have no doubt. And perhaps some of us will be keen to present copies to family members and friends...?'

When I entered the already crowded hall before the start of this morning's service, endless condolences and hugs were pressed on me; now, at its conclusion, more came my way.

'Oh my poor Mary Agnes, how will we live without our Pastor...? How will *you* cope, dear, it's so much harder for you.'

'A saint.... Latter-day saint he was...God bless him, and

God bless you, too, dear Agnes.'

'A young pastor is on his way to take over, I'm told. But, tell me, which young preacher can match the kindness and wisdom of our Pius...? Take very good care of yourself, I beseech you, Mary, do take care.'

These were people of my own neighbourhood, I've known most of them for years and years. But so drained was I by three wakeful nights of watching life ebb out of the Pastor—not to mention the wake on the following night, with its profuse readings and endless cups of tea—I barely responded to their kindness and warmth: a mere nod, a touch of the fingers...through most of it, my eyes were turned to the ground.

A few plantation workers had come, too, to pay their respects. I spotted them on the fringes of the congregation, reservedly reticent. Among them was old Thomachen, in a slightly faded black tuxedo two sizes too large for his lean frame.

Soon, Pius Philipose would be carried out to the nearby cemetery and laid six feet deep. Following a custom of Mar Thoma Christians—though as a young man, he had indeed formally broken with them when he adopted his evangelical persuasion—in his last days he specifically left instructions that he should be buried with his head to the west. So that at the end of time, when Jesus appeared in the eastern skies, and it was the hour for the dead to awaken, he would be among the first to open his eyes and greet the Saviour.

Well, to tell you the truth, I was hardly able to keep my own eyes open through the lengthy burial proceedings. Just standing upright by the pit, as they lowered the coffin, was itself a feat of endurance. All the same, having flung that clod of earth at his coffin with a resounding thud, I felt much lighter; as though in dispatching the Pastor's dead body, a great burden had been lifted off my own chest.

The kind parishioners had organized a communal potluck in his honour, a number of them contributing dry, home-cooked meat dishes, vegetable assortments and salads. The whole spread had been quietly laid out on the long table in the lounge, while hymn-singing continued inside; quite a sumptuous offering, really.

A few moments later, I accepted a plate that was handed to me, nibbled at a bit of something for form's sake, then pleading extreme fatigue, took my leave.

2

Despite sporadic showers through the night the sky remains dark and patchy.

Trees and foliage comprehensively washed turn iridescent almost as dim morning lazily penetrates a sheath of fine grey; apart from a soft drip-drip-drip, absolute silence prevails.

Where I live in the hilly region of Idukki in southern Kerala, much of the time I find great peace and quiet. This is my own home, the place I grew up in as a child. Here, the weather remains consistently cold and misty almost until noon—and, on some days, even after—never as changeable as it can be at lower altitudes.

Now an occasional grind of wheels on tarmac is heard, some delivery truck carrying supplies, or the rasp of a private motorcar labouring up endlessly undulating inclines. A delicious chill grips the air.

This morning I woke up early.

Something had disturbed my sleep: a rumbling in the tummy was it, or perhaps in my unconscious? Foolishly, my first thought was—it's Mark, returning home after all these years…. Oh no, it can't be—an intruder?

I leapt out of bed and wandered around silently, checking doors and windows. Everything was secure and bolted as it should be.

Then I climbed into bed and almost instantly fell asleep; woke up again only when the morning had turned very bright.

Today will be another strange sort of day: decidedly much too sultry for this time of year; but then everywhere the weather's become routinely unpredictable.

During my years of schooling, I spent many months at Dad's little cottage behind the main Kanjirappally market—more conveniently located for getting to school on time; but as soon as summer holidays were declared, no way you would find me anywhere except on the farm.

My vacations were filled with idleness and fun.

Every morning I would don a long white jacket and, with a toy stethoscope dangling around my neck, assume the persona of 'tree doctor': on my rounds of the infirmary, I'd patiently examine every tree trunk, every contusion or swelling of the bark, sometimes serious cases of *bleeding*, too—administering first aid wherever necessary with turmeric and a strip of cloth, or a rub down with water and scrubber. I'd then proceed to check the 'plasma' of rubber trees that had collected overnight in pots strung at their midriffs, evaluating the tree's overall health by the secretion's stickiness and consistency.

Once I had completed my rounds of the main ward, I'd spend some leisure time chatting with our glum and hoary milch goats, enquiring after their milk production, and whether they'd had a good night's sleep.

Then on to the flower beds, encouraging with a kind word and smile the newly planted yellow roses to bloom, or the wan begonias to spread abundantly.

Oh yes, there was one more chore I shouldn't forget to mention—shooing off marauding bands of monkeys with my hefty stick!

I was only twelve, and comfortably inhabited a world of my imaginings.

Well no, but I shouldn't exaggerate: the truth is I can't remember a single instance when I actually chased monkeys off our plantation—although I do remember one occasion when Achen improbably handed me a stout club, urging me to go play sentry in the spice garden.

'Monkeys!' he had warned me. 'Just watch out for those goddamn beasts! Given half a chance, they'll rip out and munch up every cardamom stalk in sight. Oh, don't they love doing that? Ten minutes! Ten minutes is all it takes them to destroy a large cardamom patch like this one. Make yourself useful, Mary, please, I'm not joking. Every able-bodied cadet has to guard against those devils.'

For a while, I took his appeal seriously—although he may only have been suggesting a novel means for coping with incipient boredom. You see, I had no companions to make my most inventive play interesting. And apart from being alone, this additional anxiety now lurked unexpressed at the back of my mind: had Dad sensibly considered how a puny twelve-year-old like me, even equipped with a heavy stick, would successfully chase away hordes of wild monkeys?

But this unresolved worry demanded no immediate assurance. So I stomped the length and breadth of our plantation, happily swinging my stick about, growling and snarling fiercely from the bottom of my throat as I chased away imaginary monkeys.

But so many years later, I had already been a widow for several months when, alone one morning, I was rudely shocked out of my wits. None of the workers, not Peter, nor Parvati had come in as yet. And then I had reason to recall Achen's words of caution.

Before I or anyone else was up and about, a monkey raid had blitzed the plantation, presumably at dawn. The attackers had vanished into thin air before anyone could assess how thoroughly they had wrecked the spice garden; confronted with disaster first thing in the morning I was stunned: a moment later, I broke down in tears.

There was a distinct drop that year, if I remember right, in Daeva Danam's income. I mean, it did result in quantifiable losses.

∽

I am alone again as so often in the recent past I have wished to be. A whole month has elapsed since my solitude was reclaimed.

Yesterday, a commemorative luncheon was held in the Pastor's honour, and his book of sermons officially released.

This time I ate very well: the tapioca-and-beef especially, with its lemony-mustardy juices, was out of this world. Molly Thomas had made it, I was told: but how did she achieve such delightful succulence? An infusion of tangerine, perhaps, instead of lemons?

Unlikely she'll ever reveal her guarded kitchen secrets to me. I suspect she doesn't like me very much.

∽

I remember how happy I once was: when I lived on this farm with my parents.

Father died many years ago. Perhaps I was responsible for breaking his heart, hastening his end. Head over heels in love with Pius I was determined to accept his hand in marriage, follow him to the ends of the world.

As it happened, we didn't have to go any great distance— only as far as Kumily—a bustling commercial town which serves as whistle-stop for tourists heading to Periyar Tiger Reserve, or pilgrims intent on Sabarimala.

In Kumily, the Mission of the Holy Spirit had provided us with rented quarters. It was an outhouse, actually, on the quiet outskirts of this noisy town.

Pius had only just been appointed assistant to another pastor, operating from nearby Cumbum, by the name of Abram Verughese. How proud he was, Pius, when that happened; as though he had finally achieved some recognition, or status in life.

In those days—why, even today—no one hears of St Thomas Christians breaking with a tradition they proudly trace back 2,000 years; yes, the Apostle is believed to have landed at Muziris, a port on the Kerala coast whose exact location is lost in antiquity. In 52 CE, Thomas arrived here by sea, converting vast numbers to the new faith. In the end, he was martyred at Mylapore, or St Thomas Mount in Chennai.

Never have I heard of any Syrian Christian voluntarily forsaking the ecumenical moorings he or she was born into; we're very proud of our ancient heritage.

But I did it: for Pius.

My parents never forgave me for being so swayed by 'that charlatan', as my father called him whenever he succumbed to his rages against his putative son-in-law. But finally, I gave my poor Dad little choice in the matter.

Myself, I was never formally 'born again' like Pius who underwent a second baptism; but gradually, I too lapsed from the Syrian Christian traditions of my own church, switching loyalties to the Mission of the Holy Spirit.

With hindsight, I might have guessed that Pius's overwhelming obsession with evangelical Protestantism arose from his knowledge that he would never be able to lead the life of celibacy that's expected of our Nazrani priests; as well as,

The Prospect of Miracles

probably, and even more decisively, his insatiable hankering after perks and bonuses that missionaries offer: good housing, travel allowance, a comfortable honorarium.

Much later, I began to suspect he may have had his eyes on Dad's place from the very start. He knew I was an only child, and my parents were rapidly ageing. After the initial rumpus I caused when I told them I wanted to marry a Protestant pastor, and the months we spent at the outhouse in Kumily, finally Pius got his way. Dad had already been dead for a few months, and Amma was too defeated to see the point in perpetuating an old quarrel over religious denomination. In any case, she was finding it difficult to manage such a large establishment on her own.

Not that she needed to for very long, in fact; only a couple of years later, she, too, passed away, and Pius and I became sole occupants of Island of the Blessed.

∽

To this day I'm slightly embarrassed by that silly name; I never use it if I have a choice.

But that's how Pius chose to arrogantly rechristen my family farm once my parents were no more.

Where was the need for that?

But he insisted on it—claiming the name had come to him in a dream, and for that reason would prove propitious.

My own forefathers had named it, more humbly, Daeva Danam, which is Malayalam for the Lord's Bounty.

∽

The house goes back three generations in my family; it's huge.

In front is a large courtyard with a well, and an enormous trellised basil creeper—until you actually see it, you would never believe a creeper can spread so densely, so riotously—providing a thick green awning for the cool underground spring that feeds our well. The gentlest of breezes makes the overgrown basil shudder and sibilate, like a garrulous yet watchful sentinel.

As with so many venerable Kerala homes, there are independent structures for the living room, storeroom, kitchen, bedroom and prayer room, each solidly constructed from timber and clay, with sloping tiled roofs. Paved pathways connect all the rooms and living spaces, a thatched canopy running overhead—clearly one large sprawling house, probably constructed incrementally over time.

A small but lucrative spice garden flourishes in the rear of the house (not so small perhaps—a little over an acre and a half) where pepper vines and cardamom shrubs have been cultivated since my grandfather's time.

An old woman cooks for me; she lives in one of the outhouses.

Another younger woman, Parvati, and her husband, Peter, are in charge of the spices. Hiring daily labourers, providing such farming inputs as they need from time to time is Peter's independent responsibility; his wife helps keep house, scouring dishes, and occasionally assisting the cook.

It's Peter who must decide every evening how many workers are required the next day—anything between twelve and twenty, I think, and settle their wages once the day's work is done. There's always so much activity on a spice plantation—more than one might imagine, and right through the year—at least *I* should have known better: I've spent so many months during school holidays every year watching Dad confabulate with his army of lieutenants—it's totally a full-time enterprise, believe me, even a small-scale venture like ours.

Dishevelling soil and turning it around after every crop is

harvested, re-fertilizing select plots, sowing seeds or saplings to the exactly prescribed depth, then daily inspection of the shrubs, nurturing, watering in case of days without rain, spraying pesticide at the first sign of any morbidity or fungus; and then the most sensitive part: estimating when exactly the produce is fully grown and ready for plucking.

Usually, it's the women who are adept at this, naturally tuned into cycles of maturity—by sheer tactile instinct as it were—merely by handling the clusters of pods they are able to pluck ones which are ripe and ready with almost no hesitation at all.

Once plucking is done—and every pod doesn't ripen at the same time as others—the little bulbs are spread out in the sun for a few hours every day before transporting sackfuls by jeep to the nearby hamlet of Murrikkady; essentially a picnic spot that draws large numbers of local tourists, it also boasts a lone, but effectively constructed furnace where most plantation owners in the region bring their produce to cure it.

Here—by prior appointment, if you please—spices are heated to a precise, calibrated temperature (*without* direct exposure to heat or flames, which is essential to maintaining the final quality), using a dual steam chamber through which steam passing through a parallel pipeline serves to mildly roast the spice over a few hours to a perfect degree of warmth.

After cardamom and pepper have been cured and cooled, they are transported back and displayed in open wicker baskets for merchants to inspect, before bidding commences on an appointed day at the Kumily Workers' Co-operative Spice Auction: a formal venue, whose vast colonnaded portico in a municipal building also serves from time to time as Town Hall for other civic events.

∽

Once the berry-like fruit is fully green, generating peppercorns involves cleaning, grinding, and packaging: a process probably less fraught than the one for cardamom which is more susceptible to the vagaries of nature. The pepper refining process is relatively mechanized, requiring less human involvement and discrimination than the one for producing high-grade cardamom. That's not to say that active supervision is not essential to every stage of maturing and curing of both spices.

On any given day you'll probably find close to fifteen or twenty workers on the plantation, both men and women. Two large, squalid huts at the extreme edge of our plot is where members of the tribal families hang out, with their aged relatives and underage children. After dark, they sometimes enjoy a drink of hooch and a meal of country fowl, and before you know it, they're fast asleep. Many live here, but not all. Essentially a floating, indeterminate population, a few actually work on nearby plantations and only occasionally come here to sleep. It's a thriving, complex and fluid community.

In previous generations their ancestors worked as bonded labour on the plantation, or put less euphemistically, as slaves. Now, with the abolition of bonded labour and governmental regulations to enforce the ban, they are more aware of their rights and undertake farm labour at a fixed daily wage.

But, in general, Adivasis whose families have been here for generations do feel somewhat entitled: as though by simple virtue of birth they have inherited a tiny plot of land their forefathers once occupied; it's too complicated and probably not even desirable to convince them otherwise, or to move for their eviction.

Besides, what would I do, in the event of Peter being unable to rope in adequate numbers on any given day?

But when it comes to those two—Peter and Parvati—I have few complaints.

Peter has some Adivasi blood in him, it's evident; Parvati probably as well, though she was an orphan, raised and educated by nuns. What's most impressive is how well they have both understood, and trained themselves to shoulder a large share of workload and responsibility on the farm; it's a boon having them around.

They don't live on the premises. They have constructed a small cottage for themselves about twenty minutes' walk down the road to Murrikkady. Nevertheless, they do spend almost their entire day on the plantation, from 8 a.m. until after dark; except Sundays, when they make it a point never to miss early morning Malayalam mass at St Jude's. I suspect their devotion to the Saint of Lost Causes has something to do with their deep longing for a child; for some obscure medical reason, Parvati is unable to conceive.

∽

Now that Pius is no more, I converse freely with myself: aloud… not all the time, but frequently.

Is something wrong with me? I'm not at all ashamed of a habit I've indulged since the time I was just four or five—a fervid mental life made it most natural for me to discuss matters with myself; besides, so often I was the only friend I had. I continue to be that even today without feeling in the least bit self-conscious; my own friend, that is.

But *he* disapproved: Pius frowned at this harmless, childish idiosyncrasy of mine. When he first discovered it—overheard me talking to myself, that is—he showed excessive concern, grave solicitude, as though he had caught me yielding to a secret vice.

He deplored it as weakness of mind, an unhealthy kink in my constitution, begged me to control myself.

Later, he showed annoyance, annoyance that quickly turned to anger.

A 'pathetic lack of self-control' is how he described it, and it irritated him no end that my conversations with myself implied I could be so preoccupied, so terribly self-enclosed—to his own exclusion, of course—in fact, according to *his* sagacious estimate I was actually mentally distraught, if not downright disturbed. Whenever he overheard me saying something to myself, he would shake his head and stalk off, filled as it were with unbearable despair, disgust or indignation, I can't say which it was.

Once, I even spied him twirling his index finger at his temple as he walked away, as if elucidating to himself that a screw had slipped loose somewhere in one's upper storey! I suppose it could just as well have been an expression of his own despair? Or more likely, he probably *wanted* me to observe that vile gesture: never did care to shield me from hurtful innuendoes, did he?

And if indeed I *had* seen him, taken note of his withering contempt, it would have meant little more to him than yet another milestone in his campaign to carefully cultivate seeds of self-doubt in the forecourt of my mind.

But why am I persisting with these destructive memories? They do make me angry, but somewhat fluttery also, and unsure of myself.

His preoccupation with my behaviour was a devious stratagem for controlling and oppressing me, I'm pretty certain of that now, for insinuating and tampering with the very mental well-being for which he claimed such concern.

But then, I never once dared articulate as much to him— how could I have, I'm still not fully convinced it's true—and there was always that look of studied innocence and boundless compassion with which he trumped every argument we ever had, making me doubt, even despise myself.

Why do I keep harking back to those difficult moments in our marriage?

There were just as many grand days at the beginning—during our betrothal, our solemn, conjugal union, when I felt his love for me as something real, that completely reciprocated my own.

Those first months were so uncomplicatedly happy. I sometimes wonder if they were no more than a fleeting dream.

Now that he's dead and gone—and we Malayalis have a weakness for this, I suspect, you might call it a 'holier-than-thou' regional complicity—many parishioners are inclined to aggrandize and glorify him as a 'saint'. Among them, I believe, a small, self-important cabal has even sent a petition to the Vatican appealing for his beatification!

O Lord! I do believe. But help thou my disbelief! I, his wife of so many years know one thing for certain: this Pius who so wholeheartedly embraced his Mission of the Holy Spirit while still alive, harboured but one deadly intent in his heart: he would never rest in peace until he had ensured that that his wife's self-esteem was in tatters.

It was all rather surreptitiously done I must say, this move, I mean, to beatify him. Heard of it from an acquaintance who mentioned it casually, assuming I already knew. But that was the first I'd heard of it.

I suppose the sanctimonious lot that initiated this supplication to the Pope must also consider me an unworthy wife for the late Pastor; and possibly, if they chose to credit certain rumours flying around for a while, a woman of decidedly loose morals!

3

When I first met Pius, I don't believe it had occurred to him as yet to take refuge in the cloth.

He belonged to a Syrian Christian family that had practically no land holdings left; only his mother, a retired schoolteacher, was still alive at the time. His father, a hard drinker, had disposed of most of their land piecemeal to support his habit and then dropped dead one morning at breakfast when he choked on a splinter of bone in a pork sandwich he was gobbling down.

Despite setbacks such as these in his younger days, Pius somehow acquired a little practical knowledge of plumbing and a basic training in electrical wiring. At the time, he was trying to set himself up as a contractor, soliciting freelance jobs in these trades.

Well, perhaps to earn an honest living by the sweat of his brow was not to his taste at all.

Can't say what hurdles or obstacles beset him that made him switch careers so dramatically, but when next I ran into him, he invited me to join a small group of do-gooders on a visit to an orphanage in Angamaly.

It was December and the purpose of our visit was to distribute presents to the orphans ahead of Christmas, something to gladden their dismal lives. I had little else better to do and went along in a hired minibus. Only towards the end of that long and resolutely cheery day, after other folks had been dropped off at convenient points near their homes, Pius and I stopped for a cup of tea in a small cafe.

It was then he told me he had joined the evangelical Mission of the Holy Spirit.

I asked what had inspired him to disavow the St Thomas Christians his family had always belonged to.

'For more than 2,000 years,' he explained, 'St Thomas Christians have remained faithful to the Apostle's teaching. But now, as we approach the end of an epoch, it is time to take stock of what Jesus himself had to say about our times.'

And after a brief pause, he quoted from memory,

'"Verily, said Jesus to Nicodemus, a leader of the Jews, verily I say unto thee, except a man be born again, he cannot see the kingdom of God. And Nicodemus asked him how a man can be born again when he is old? Can he enter his mother's womb again? And Jesus replied he has to be born again of water and the Holy Spirit."

'Every prophecy in the Bible indicates that we are certainly living in end times now. Every true believer knows how important it is to spread the Word of the Lord to every corner of the world, preparing the way for His Second Coming.'

Unless my memory is playing tricks with me, when he was younger, Pius's complexion was actually a few shades lighter. With those long, impossibly tangled curls bedecking his crown he was a gorgeous man. He was twelve years older than me which, when they first heard I wanted to marry him, had alarmed my parents. But, to me, he seemed just as young as I was, a fine partner for life. Later, he grew dark and stout, lost most of his hair and was compelled to trim what remained very short; his facial skin had turned coarse and wrinkled, marked by tiny purulent eruptions.

Yet those piercing eyes remained, just as riveting.

Pius sipped his tea, frowned, and continued, 'But most of all, what convinced me to throw in my lot with the Mission was a dream I had; repeatedly, over several consecutive nights.' And he described to me the dream that had convinced him of his priestly vocation so late in life.

He told me how on the morning after the first night's dreaming, he had felt strangely moved; yet could not understand why the dream should have touched him so deeply. But night after night, as soon as he fell asleep the same dream recurred with minor variations, and he realized God was trying to say something to him.

He was standing on the summit of a hill overlooking a beautiful green meadow, there was nobody in sight for miles, he was alone and feeling quite perplexed. What on earth was he doing there? Before him, scattered over the vast undulating stretch of green, roamed a large flock of sheep. At first, he looked around, scanning the fuzzy dots on the carpet of grass for any sign of a shepherd boy slouching in the distance, or napping under the shade of a plane tree. But there seemed none about.

As the dream recurred, with clockwork persistence, a clear knowledge dawned on him—and he said he knew this even in his sleep, while still dreaming, this he claimed was its most amazing feature—the flock of sheep he was gazing at belonged to God, and that it was he, Pius, who was the shepherd boy. It was he who was supposed to tend to them. A direct message from God it was, he felt, that he should devote his life to being a pastor.

Typically, when Pius approached the local office of the Mission, he didn't attempt to hide the fact—nor brazenly advertise it—that he had been convinced by a nocturnal vision of his true calling.

After an initial training period which didn't last longer than a few months, he was appointed by the Mission as assistant pastor to Abram Verughese.

If I think back to the time when Pius was courting me, while simultaneously launching his career as pastor, I cannot help being struck by how deliberate and scheming the course of both courtship and career were. But that's not how I saw it then: I was fairly swept off my feet by his charm, energized and excited by the vision, drive and ingenuity of this inspired young pastor-to-be who, besides everything else, happened to be the first man to ever have shown any romantic interest in me.

That romantic interest, I have to admit, didn't endure for long. But I didn't hold this against him. After all, he had become so busy with his new calling.

How seriously he took it I could only observe in silent amazement: remoulding his personality, it seemed to me, he was presenting himself to the world as morally unblemished, upright, drenched in the milk of human kindness...completely earnest in every respect. In other words, cultivating an image that was fully in consonance with the stature of his new office: Pastor, albeit assistant.

∽

As I have said, it was Dad, Appa Jacko as he was called by everyone in Kanjirappally, who remained most unimpressed by the flamboyant Pius.

Dad's real name was Chacko Daniel. But so widely known was his admiration for Michael Jackson, the late pop star whose songs and videos still created a sensation on TV every time they were aired, that the shared sobriquet had stuck. The singing and dancing star was probably twenty years or more his junior, but Dad was hip and forward-thinking enough to feel totally transported by Jackson's talent and creativity. In his younger days, I remember, when he was more agile, he even managed a fair if slightly amusing version of the former's silky, lissom 'moonwalk'.

When it came to Pius, Dad decided almost as soon as he had met him that the man was a 'humbug', a spiritual pretender. Many years later, I would learn the dislike had been mutual.

My mother, on the other hand, Amma Rosalie, was more like me, a woman taken in by his curly locks and expansive charms, in the end she grew rather fond of Pius. Months after Dad had passed away, at Amma Rosalie's invitation we moved back to Daeva Danam.

Soon, Pius began to assert a masculine authority over the establishment, implying by his ways that only a man could know how to properly maintain and expeditiously run a large farmhouse. Oh yes, ostensibly, it was also to make life easier for Amma, save her the routine hassles. And initially Amma protested the rate at which he was usurping every responsibility and useful chore she had previously performed herself.

He was very hard-working, I'll say that for him. Pius seemed to have enough time for everything, supervising as well as participating in the assiduous hive of activity that's farm life— from cultivation, harvesting and marketing of spices, upkeep of the small vegetable patch we still maintain for domestic use, having the water in our well cleaned once in every six months, not to mention rearing and fussing after two goats that Amma had adopted at the time, which gave enough milk for the family's consumption.

I am inclined to believe in some subliminal way Pius sensed that to deprive her of every bit of bustle which gave her life purpose and meaning was one infallible way to ensure she didn't live too long.

Sure enough, by the time Pastor Abram Verughese came to lunch at the invitation of his assistant for a private blessing and renaming of the farmhouse, Amma Rosalie was already quite ill and wasting away. Of course, it's only fair I put on record that Pius spared no expense or effort to get her the very best treatment. When the local medical fraternity made little headway, he arranged for doctors from as far away as Kollam and Coimbatore to visit us and ply her with their medicines, he even resorted to folk nostrums in the end.

But there's not much that can bring around an old woman who knows she's not needed anymore. Amma Rosalie's illness, never conclusively diagnosed, continued to impair and oppress her for over three years; this was a difficult period for me and a very busy one for Parvati; from being a person so active, preoccupied and personally responsible for so much, my mother found herself changed in a relatively short time into an old, arthritic and helpless woman; never going out, never leaving her room, and towards the end, entirely bedridden. Once she passed away, Pius and I had only each other for company on the Island of the Blessed and, of course, there was little Mark, who had just completed three. It was then I felt my first twinge of irrational fear. Would I be able to live here alone with Pius?

My son had been born while we were still living in the outhouse in Kumily, with only a midwife in attendance. Shortly after we had moved back to the farm, he started to go to a playschool and then kindergarten. Through all his years of schooling I was kept very busy. But once he grew up, developed a mind of his own, he left home. It became another reason to feel afraid I wouldn't be able to cope.

4

He had an odd way of creeping up on me to see what I was up to.

Perhaps he merely wanted to ascertain if I was still talking to myself, something he had strictly forbidden.

Do it for my sake, Pius had urged, even if you don't believe you need to do it for your own. He had warned it could lead to complete mental breakdown. He even went so far, on another occasion, as to suggest there was something 'unholy' about it, that Satan had a sly way of interloping the space offered by weak minds.

Within myself, I laughed at the idea—privately, I had begun to laugh at so many things Pius said and did. On many occasions I couldn't help recall my father's parodying of his pompous ways—which until the very end Pius himself seemed blissfully unselfconscious about.

Talking aloud was an old habit of mine, one I was perfectly comfortable with—I couldn't refrain from it entirely. But now if I spoke to myself, I did it ever so softly, and without moving my lips. And another thing: I always kept an ear out for approaching footsteps.

Nevertheless, when he crept up on me like that to watch or eavesdrop on me, he only succeeded in giving me a terrible start. I was in the kitchen, and I yelled at him.

'Why do you snoop around like that? You gave me such a fright!'

'Snoop around?'

'So silently.... I didn't even know you were back.'

'I'm sorry if I startled you, Mary,' he apologized sheepishly. 'Didn't mean to at all…. Just stopped by to ask…will lunch will be ready soon? I have to go out again—'

'I'm quite alone in the kitchen, as you can see. Poor Mariamma was running a fever all of last night and this morning, too, until I made her swallow some paracetamol and sent her back to bed. Lunch will be ready soon…in about fifteen, twenty minutes?'

'Oh, good. Then I can eat a bit before pushing off—'

'Where to now? Again? In this heat…?'

'There's work to be done, my dear. I'm meeting Abram at the town office. From there we'll be taking the jeep to Kumbalangi. A suspected case of possession has been reported.'

'Ha-ha…' I smirked. 'So Abram is going to play exorcist?'

'No. Well, probably not today. Today we'll only try to find out more, investigate. Verify if the case is genuine….'

Was I being deliberately provocative when I suggested, 'Psychological distress, more likely, don't you think?'

'A young schoolgirl is behaving in obdurately filthy ways, and spouting Latin phrases at her parents to boot, ' Pius retaliated sarcastically, 'but of course, Madam Psychiatrist knows the case much better, without even meeting her patient…'

'I'm just saying. We are not living in the Middle Ages.'

'No, we're not. But then, if we *are* living in the end times—and as you know, in the last 2,000 years, every prophecy contained in the Bible has turned out to be one hundred per cent accurate—the Bible also predicts that the evil one will become hyperactive in this current era. We see evidence of it all around us, don't we? Social unrest, earthquakes, natural calamities…. Cases of possession simply cannot—and should not—be dismissed as unlikely, or outlandish.'

'Point taken, Pastor. My apologies….'

'Ah, yes…thank you. As yet only a humble assistant,' Pius smiled. 'And now that I consider it, a quite famished one, may I confess?'

'Of course, dear, you must eat before going out. Just give me five minutes, only the rice remains to be done,' I said, turning my attention back to the pot bubbling on the gas. 'Fish curry's all ready….'

'Great!'

When I think of those first years at Kumily, or even later, the time after we moved back to the farm, I don't doubt at all that Pius and I were very much in love. Hardly a moment, or an hour away from each other, and the languorous ache of separation made itself acutely felt, only to be soothed, as swiftly we flew into each other's arms again.

∽

Even so, married life with Pius, initiated at an outhouse in a sleepy suburb of Kumily, I have to admit, wasn't everything one could have wished for.

Don't get me wrong, I'm not complaining about the accommodation: a simple but reasonably well-furnished outhouse attached to a stately, turreted mansion (on long-term lease to the Holy Spirit Mission), whose deacon for South Asia, an American, hadn't visited Kerala in over two years; also resident on the vast wooded property was a friendly caretaker couple whose presence I was often rather glad for—they occupied another smaller lodge some distance away from ours.

The truth was I yearned for Daeva Danam, even though our lodgings were about as close an alternative as I could have hoped for.

More than anything else, I missed my parents terribly. I realized how much I must have hurt them with my obstinately impetuous behaviour. My feelings of guilt were at first amply assuaged by the novelty and adventure of my situation with Pius—it was almost an elopement we had pulled off, although we were located no more than forty kilometres away, and I kept in touch with Amma on the phone.

But I soon realized, as my parents had repeatedly tried to caution me, that the great passion I felt for Pius was largely unexamined; I would have to start living with him before I was able to understand that I just didn't know him well enough.

In every respect a self-assured, well-spoken and grandiloquent man; oddly, these admirable traits were the very things about him that began to grate on me. As for the relative peace and energizing pleasures of those early years, I can only attribute them to Pius's resolute efforts to instil me with child—and the actual months of my pregnancy—which despite every indication to the contrary convinced me he really cared.

More excitement less anxiety did Pius show through my entire confinement than I myself did, entirely assured as he was of its eventual outcome: a son he had prayed for, a son he was confident God would send us.

We weren't disappointed: Mark: Pius' choice of name, at once charming and apt—I was relieved for once he didn't claim the name had come to him in a dream!—was a delightfully energetic infant who giggled and raced on all fours through endless heaps of wet, stinky nappies unruffled by bouts of colic, raging catarrh and whatnot; determined as though never to cause displeasure to his parents. So much so that Pius, who seldom let pass any occasion to display his egregiously sketchy acquaintance with world religions compared Mark's innate good nature to the nursling Zarathustra's irrepressible levity, the cherubic Lao Tse's unshakeable graciousness.

∽

Everything had been a lot different in the days just after I became pregnant.

Pius was more considerate then, made efforts to show how much he cared. This improved state of relations continued, and was further invigorated by Mark's birth, and during his infancy. He loved Mark very much and took great pride in his precocity, his astonishing intelligence. But that's how most parents feel about their kids while they are still young, isn't it?

The brief moments of tenderness between father and son didn't last long. Very soon, Pius—now a full-time pastor—became busier with his parish work, and was rarely at home.

Later on in life—that was so much later, of course—father and son developed great antipathy: Mark simply couldn't stand Pius. When he was nineteen, he found a job in Delhi and went away. He has been back only once for a period of just fifteen days that he spent with us on the farm; never since. I do miss him very much.

For a while, he stayed in touch. I had an address I could write to. Then he moved out of that place, and even my letters stopped reaching him. The ones that came back had the legend rubber-stamped on them: *Addressee not found.* I tried only once more when his father died to write again, with no more than a grain of hope that my sad tidings and the postal services would find a way to penetrate his intractable isolation.

5

Was there something faintly macabre about Pius's predecessor?

I liked to pretend this was so, though admittedly with a large pinch of mirth.

Withered and prematurely aged, Abram was victim to hyper hirsutism: an unfortunate disorder of the hormonal glands that was responsible for an extraordinary amount of hair all over his body. Chest and neck, of course, but saucer-shaped ears, too, from each of which mushroomed large tufts, not to mention a soft downy fleece that carpeted his arms and covered him all the way to the tips of his fingers and toes. An odd figure, indeed, whose dense growth gave him a curiously brutish appearance.

But Verughese's woes didn't end there: several years ago, while negotiating uneven terrain he lost his footing and crashed face first into a rock!

Half a dozen careful extractions later, our local orthodontist created a removable denture for Abram which he found so excruciatingly painful to use he often forgot to slip it on. In the reverend's presence thus, one was bestowed with sporadic glimpses of a startlingly cavernous maw in which receding gums created a craggy backdrop to three prominent, needle-sharp canines—associations with vampiric craving became unavoidable.

Ha-ha.... Such idle daydreaming, these days it helps me

pass the time. Isn't the quotidian fiercely bizarre? And incredibly funny too, besides?

Now I'm alone, I not only discuss matters with myself a great deal more, but also—no doubt Pius would be appalled to learn this—chuckle, or even laugh aloud frequently!

But jokes apart, Verughese was a gentle soul of whom we grew very fond in the years he served our community. In the face of mounting ill-health, general debility and compounded dental affliction, he felt it best to resign as pastor and move back to his village near Devikulam, in the highlands of Malanad.

What a valediction parishioners gave him: a ceremonial mass, a grand, limitless feast: Kanjirappally's innumerable beggars, and countless others from villages around, went home that afternoon substantially sated on the appetizing contents of two steaming cauldrons filled to the brim with spicy shrimp biryani and shallots, served with pineapple raita.

When the send-off for the retiring pastor was winding down, and the last of the stragglers had wiped the great pots clean, one of the parishioners who had brought his car and driver with him, offered to transport Abram and his luggage to Devikulam, or even all the way to Marayoor, his village. But the retiring pastor demurred, saying he had already sent off many of his effects by bus last week, and now had only one suitcase to carry. He would feel more comfortable if he caught the 5 p.m. local bus, as he usually did whenever he needed to travel to Marayoor.

After bidding everyone goodbye, the pastor said a last few words to his incumbent successor. He hugged him warmly several times and held him in an embrace for long minutes. I was close enough to listen to the words he muttered in his ear.

'Pius, my dear Pius…by retiring prematurely as I am, I am doing you a terrible disservice….'

'How so, Pastor?' asked Pius, stepping back.

'In abandoning the parishioners to your as yet inexperienced care....'

'Oh no, no Pastor,' said Pius. 'You're giving me a fine chance to learn and grow...and I'm certain I will bring you credit, honour the noble tradition you have so firmly established. There's no need at all, Pastor, for any guilty feeling.... After so many years of unselfish devotion, you deserve to see to your own health now, and that of your near and dear ones. Your aged aunty must be very old, and missing you.'

'Thanks, my dear boy...I appreciate what you just said.' The two pastors were once again clinched in a firm embrace.

'May the Lord bless all your endeavours....'

'I am not alone, Pastor,' Pius added. 'I have my wife with me, my little son, and the parishioners themselves don't forget to inspire me...to teach me.... You take care, Pastor Abram.'

'God bless you, son....'

∽

Thanks to Pius, already familiar to his parishioners, and waiting in the wings for his promotion, the transition was effected rather smoothly.

Once he had become head pastor of Jerusalem Hosanna Church, Pius came into his own.

To begin with, all I mean by that—and indeed it was all I knew at the time—he donned the role of pastor with fierce resolve. Soon acknowledged as an inspiring 'model' of selfless ministry, he never spared himself when it came to service of his flock.

Or so he was universally regarded. But I was in the unique position of being able to observe him from very close.

At about the time of his investiture—and this is an indelible impression I can never forget—so distinctly pleased was he by his elevated status that he actually put on kilos of flab; his face grew puffy, if not puffed-up. I remember I had to get the family tailor to alter two of his trousers at the waist!

And then, something undeniably sinister emerged as well.

This bizarre and alarming side of him became evident to me the more he relished the eminence accorded him by humble parishioners. Of course, it also frightened me.

It was a face that Pius flashed only once in a while—dark and keenly edged; and almost never in front of outsiders—even Amma with whom we were living in the same farmhouse was probably unaware of its existence.

Call it an intemperate anger, if you like, terrifying for its suddenness and intensity.

Well, you could say that by virtue of his position he did exert strong moral authority over our small community. But his diatribes, when directed at an alcoholic husband or an undutiful son, were always delivered in rather a preachy, compassionate, sometimes even appeasingly jocular idiom: tipplers, layabouts, wife beaters—the handful of irresponsible souls endemic to any semi-rural community—were scolded rather gently, as though seeking not to ruffle feathers, or create enduring alienation.

What I'm about to tell you, though—and I won't mince words describing my relationship with the Pastor—was enacted exclusively between him and me, and only when we were alone together—the full demonic face of his anger rose to the surface and possessed him: often without my being able to comprehend what I had done to bring on myself his rages.

No, perhaps I'm not getting this right: there was anger, I'm sure—I couldn't but sense it at every mundane turn of domestic events—yet it was never explosive or of intemperate nature, but one that remained always suppressed, bottled-up. He never gave vent to his displeasure or unhappiness, never raved or ranted. But his facial muscles became tense and impassive, his piercing eyes froze stonily, and his nostrils—his nostrils flared and quivered uncontrollably. At times, his eyebrows rose in astonishment. As if he couldn't for the life of him believe he had actually married this woman.

I puzzled over it a great deal, but couldn't discuss it with anybody else. As far as the general public went, Pius was a caring and compassionate pastor. No one, absolutely no one would have believed me had I complained he was prone to fits of sudden irascibility.

But I should clarify right away: intimidating as his anger could be, never once did he raise his hand on me—no, he wasn't that crude. Yet, even while his attacks remained entirely verbal and seemingly subdued, I could feel seething beneath his words a vehemence barely short of physical assault.

What became of the love between us that had convinced me I should marry this man? What did I do to lose it? My desperation to find an answer to this enigma often reached fever pitch, especially when I was alone. I would break down in tears of self-doubt, incomprehension.

There were days when I felt I was walking on brittle ground—on eggshells!—as though fearful I might, without realizing it, pulverize something terribly fragile. While Mark was still growing up, travelling to school and back every day, there was plenty to keep me preoccupied, both parents, in fact, as well as delighted and charmed. Children are so undeniably magical. Whatever the cause of the unhappiness between us, Pius and I had tacitly decided never to refer to it overtly, or with any truthfulness—

especially never in Mark's presence.

Difficult it was for me to anticipate at all times what I had done that he disapproved of, something that in his eyes was irresponsible, foolish or morally degenerate. But on just those very days when I was feeling like that, as if deliberately to put me at ease and prove my fears baseless, he could be so charmingly friendly, I would wonder if I was in fact—as he had so often claimed in the recent past—suspicious of him to a point of depressive paranoia?

Often, I was compelled to wonder, was he deliberately terrorizing me? As some trial of strength in which both were pitted against the other; yet only one fully versed in the inflexible rules of the game? Or was he victim himself to some unidentified illness that on occasion raised his blood to boiling point and drove him virtually insane?

The most insignificant irritations could spark off his choler, such as an unavoidable variation in his otherwise rigid schedule, or some perceived infringement of 'orthodox' practice on my part. Ironic, of course, that having broken with the more traditional Syrian Christian church, Pius should have espoused even greater fundamentalism when he joined hands with the evangelicals. But more than that, I often wondered to what extent it was repressed anger against his own wife that bubbled and fermented within him—suddenly to spill over with so much latent, undeclared fury.

Later, other explanations for his behaviour occurred to me—vague insinuations, wispy innuendos that floated to my ears and shocked me—outlandishly unthinkable ones, of course. Nevertheless, if dwelled upon, they did offer a plausible if devilish explanation for my Pastor's aggressive incontinence.

I knew I wasn't, not by any excess of imagination, crazy. Yet I had a duty to myself to investigate. And somehow I knew this would involve raising a matter with Parveen: beseeching greater candour from her about a chance remark she had once made to me. Even at the time, years ago, it had only been hearsay: Pius and I were then engaged to be married, you see, so all talk of his shady past sounded laughable—no more than a reason to be annoyed with wicked rumour-mongering by envious people.

6

In a clear, colourless sky, wisps of grey smudge drift listlessly for days.

No evidence of cloud accumulation, or signs of impending rainfall. Then, late that evening, fierce thunder, delirious lightning, and of a sudden a darkly garbled sky splits open and gushes for hours.

Much cooler this morning, wouldn't you say?

Air diaphanous, that deeply comforting smell of moist earth everywhere: but it won't last. Already the sky is dazzlingly bright, and getting hotter with every passing hour. I sit in my living room quite alone, wondering what's become of that bitch Parveen?

හ

Impossible that she couldn't have heard of Pius's passing.

I had thought since she missed the funeral she would certainly be there for the seventh day, mind. But no, a month later, though the release of his book of sermons was announced on three parish notice boards across the city, she's nowhere to be seen. And now, four months later I still have no news of Parveen.

While Pius was around it was difficult enough; decidedly awkward for her to visit me, or for us to stay in touch even by phone. He had made it clear he didn't approve. If he was home, he would rush to answer the phone every time it rang: keeping track, I had assumed, of what calls I was receiving. Who would've dreamt Pastor was anxious I shouldn't answer his private calls?

Myself, I hardly receive any calls even today; but I did have this one friend whom he so disliked, and made his disaffection evident to—on those few occasions when they happened to meet by chance.

Why did it have to be like that? Why was he so formal and severe, so controlling? How many years have flown by! His upbringing in a hidebound and austere Mar Thoma Christian tradition, with its rules for days of fasting, prayer, harsh proscription of any form of entertainment, be it reading novels, going to the cinema or turning on the television set—wait a moment, I don't think he was ever allowed one at home—would have conditioned his entire outlook on the future.

And his reasons for not accepting my friendship with Parveen? Never did figure them out—perhaps because she was Muslim? That one fact made her an unlikely subject for proselytization, which was the one grand project of his later life.

Not that he ever tried to influence her beliefs, not in my presence at least. But his opinions about her religion and its 'fanatical hordes', though never expressed to her face, were as clear as daylight for all who knew him. And besides, he was completely convinced himself, wasn't he, that anyone who hoped to be saved on that final Day of Revelation had better embrace Jesus right now?

Oh no, I understood much later: what irked Pius most was that my relationship with Parveen was exclusive, harking back to a time well before I became so much as acquainted with him. And, of course, he must have sensed how intimate we had once been.

That I should have such a dear friend was intolerable to him;

it went against the very core of his nature which demanded he be positioned at the hub of all his relationships.

Well, now he's gone for good. So why the hell is this woman still behaving strangely, so stand-offish with me?

⸸

At high school, Parveen and I were very close. From the moment we reached Loyola Convent until the end of the day, inseparable.

In many classrooms we sat beside each other sharing one desk. After school, when I got picked up in my father's car she would often climb in with me, and get dropped off en route. But even more frequently, we'd tell Ravi, Dad's driver, to head straight back to the farm. That was our preferred routine.

She was practically living with us, for days on end. One shelf of my wardrobe was reserved for her clothes, another in my study for her schoolbooks. If there was homework to be done, we'd work at it together, wrap it up as quickly as possible. Then, all evening muck around the plantation, playing games we'd ourselves invented.

One, I remember, in particular, was a great favourite with both of us.

I would enact the role of wealthy plantation owner, and she, Parveen, would be my slave: attentive to every whim and fancy whether verbally expressed or not: the essence of the game was that she had to be able to guess my mind accurately, or bear the penalty of my displeasure. Of course, this latter was calculated in points and forfeits; only a game, but one that allowed me to indulge my sadistic impulses considerably.

Several times I did offer that we switch places. She could be princess of the plantation, sovereign, or whatever it was I was playing, and I would be her slave instead: but Parveen preferred subservience. And in a way, she was so genuinely sweet-natured, so compliant—my one true childhood friend—I felt she fitted the part of slave to a T, so I let her keep it, and enjoyed being the overbearing landlord.

At that tender age, too, sexual awareness hovered undeniably in our consciousness like an unripened fruit waiting to be plucked, although, in specifics, we knew so little. I do remember an underlying thrill that radiated through our game. Parveen's role as slave encompassed not so much the physical work she undertook for me—that too, of course: mixing manure into soil, pulling out weeds, tilling the field, or cooking us a tasty meal—much of this performed and credited for only in the imagining—but its dominant delight was that prurient itch, the seductive power I knew I could exercise over my guileless girlfriend: only the two of us complicit in our relationship, and Parveen cheerfully acquiescing to every condition: which made her, I suppose, apart from everything else my willing sexual slave as well.

The small cot under my bed, fitted with casters, created a terrific rumble every time we pulled it out; so thunderous, it was heard all over the farm. Once that rumble was declared, it was a cue for servants to make the bed, provide clean sheets, a cover and pillow for Parveen. I remember Kishori offering often enough to oil the casters, but never getting down to doing it.

After darkness enveloped the farmhouse, and the lights were switched off, my sweet friend climbed into my own queen-sized bed, in preference to her pygmy cot, and our games would continue. We slept in each other's arms, whispering until late into the night; and she made me feel a queen: cuddling and caressing, touching me all over; and I would kiss her mouth hard, her smooth hairless face passionately, imbibing and sucking of her so deeply, as though she were the juice of a delicious fruit I must consume entirely before sleep commanded our eyes shut.

We were in love, Parveen and I, or at least enjoyed pretending we were.

As it happened, she had five younger brothers and sisters whom her mother was busy looking after. She had little time to think of Parveen's whereabouts; although, she probably did know quite well, and was secretly pleased that her eldest offspring had found much favour with the venerable Nazrani family at the plantation of Daeva Danam—she had practically been inducted into their household.

My parents never objected to Parveen's sleeping over, or living with us for days on end. They were happy I had found a 'sibling'. It was my mother's greatest regret that I never had one, and both of them thought Parveen a very nice girl.

Now Parveen herself is proud mother to two grown-up sons, one eighteen, the other twenty.

∽

When we tired of our vicarious, make-believe games in the estate garden, we simply shifted to its periphery; a fascinatingly rudimentary sort of place, Kishori's hut. Here we plumped cross-legged on the caked, cow-dung floor.

Sipping hot, full-cream coffee which she never failed to whip up for us in a jiffy, we allowed our minds to wander into other worlds, other versions of reality which, if not completely invented like our own games, were no less alien or fantastic: life in the thick forests of Attappady, trapping and hunting various animals, skinning, then roasting them on open fires, an abundant supply of meat fuelling night-long dances, further animated by large clay pots of toddy and delicious (so we imagined) home-brewed country liquor.

We heard more sombre stories too—about greedy, government officials and policemen, gun-toting ganja-cultivating mafia gangs, manipulative traders who made it their business to illegally purchase plots of reserved forest land, further exploiting the tribes by haggling mercilessly over the price they were willing to offer for painstakingly accumulated heaps of forest produce; all these human specimens pressurizing, if not terrorizing, the indigenous forest dwellers, and their tiny, diminishing villages. Simple shepherds, that's what the name Kurumba actually means—a far cry, from that other era ages ago, when they were known as fierce warriors of resilient antiquity, dreaded by every other tribe. The stories we enjoyed most pertained to that fabulous, long vanished past when powerful Kurumba sorcerers, diviners, exorcists and medicine men ruled the roost.

∽

Attappady province was but a five-hour bus ride away from Kanjirappally, although after the bus had dropped her off on the highway, Kishori would proceed north on foot for another three hours through thick forest before she reached her ooru, or village, which was called Edavani. And, of course, she would be carrying her little moppet with her: Nirmala, born eight years before I came into the world.

Having a child to take care of didn't deter Kishori from making this difficult journey fairly often: once a year for a month and a half, or two, she would go home to meet her husband and her ageing father-in-law. But her husband, attacked by a wild boar during a hunt, succumbed to a wound in his thigh which turned gangrenous, leaving Kishori a widow just three years into their marriage.

When I was born, Nirmala was already growing up on our

farm, much faster, it seemed to me, than I was.

Parveen and I soaked in every story that Kishori told us: at times, bitter and gruesome ones, at others, resigned and fateful others: stories of deprivation and dispossession, of the unstoppable and unending plunder of a great forest heritage. Once her husband died, and later his father, Kishori stopped making those yearly excursions to Edavani.

There was an ancient Kurumba folktale she often told us.

There was a sorcerer, many years ago, who would come to the villages of the Kota tribe, kill all the Kota men and sleep with all their beautiful women....

The dwindling Kota men were much agitated by this and one day waylaid the black Kurumba in the forest and cut him to pieces. They cut off his arms and legs and threw them in every direction. But just as they were returning happily to their villages, telling each other how good it was to be rid of the black Kurumba at last, there he was, standing in their path at the crossroads, doubling up with laughter.

'Oh, so you thought it would be so easy to get rid of me, did you…let's see then?'

Then followed the terrifying vengeance of the sorcerer whose rollicking and guffawing overwhelmed the villagers: at first with shrieks of infectious risibility—they all seemed to be having a good laugh—but which soon became uncontrollable, the whole pack of Kota tribesmen racked by spasms of unendurable laughter-agony, which made them quake and whoop, flung them this way and that. Soon, their helpless cackling, no longer exultant or funny, became laceratingly intense and bruising: it went on and on like that until, suffocating, hysterically wrecked, they collapsed and died on the spot.

In the story, I remember, there was also a talking parrot, who was the sorcerer himself, in feathered form. And the sorcerer's jealous, scheming, but also lascivious wife who had an appetite for men. An incredible ease of narration informed Kishori's storytelling, and the fable evolved intricately every time she told it, growing in unexpected ways and along improbable axes, a living, breathing creature that never fully reached culmination, even as shadows lengthened in the spice fields outside and we received our summons for dinner.

At one time, centuries ago, according to Kishori, Kurumba was the dominant tribe of the region. Their powers were believed to be so effective that others feared and respected them. Alleged supernatural misdeeds by the Kurumbas in the 1800s caused a massacre of retaliation from other tribes in the Nilgiris—so entrenched was the belief in the power of Kurumba sorcery.

∽

It was Kishori, Nirmala's mother, whom my Dad had 'rescued' from serious illness and brought home from the forests of Attappady, after a hunting expedition. He was a young man then.

My Dad fancied guns and himself as an intrepid hunter. Although often enough he came home empty-handed with no more than a civet cat or a monitor lizard to show for his bravado, Attappady was a region he enjoyed visiting as often as he could take time off from the farm, with one or two of his hunting cronies. They would drive there in an open jeep with a big flashlight, set up camp and hunt. Once or twice, he did bring home bigger game—a stag or a wild hog, but this was relatively infrequent.

On one such hunting trip, Dad had been provided a roof over his head—a thatched hut—for himself and his pals by the headman of a tribal hamlet called Edavani; not to mention, large amounts of toddy, liquor, cooked and salted meats, yams, nuts and other locally produced delicacies.

No doubt the moopan of the tribal hamlet, who had provided these services, was compensated handsomely for them, for my Dad was known to be a very generous man.

But it was the headman's cousin, Kunjam Pillai, the village bandari, or accountant, who was given a reason for life-long gratitude to Dad. My Dad was able to save his last surviving family member from almost certain dehydration and death.

'If a child fell sick in our village,' Kishori had once told us, 'it was the beginning of a long and hazardous trek....'

The men cut a bamboo shaft to which they tied a blanket to make a hammock. A team was formed: the fittest among the men ran ahead, while the others took turns carrying the sick child. The journey from the ooru to the Mudur Primary Health Centre was eighteen kilometres. The men had to traverse the Edavani foothills, where they had to watch out for wild bears that knocked down rocks from the hillocks.

If it was night, they travelled by instinct, guided by the distant hoots of the runner. If the Varagar was overflowing, they had to forget about finding medical assistance for the invalid—child or adult—they couldn't start out at all.

Kunjam Pillai had lost both his wife and a firstborn infant to cholera only five years ago in just such circumstances. And now it appeared that his four-year-old may have caught the bug, too, besides suffering malnutrition. Contaminated drinking water was a serious problem in the area. Flash floods caused by the overflowing river had cut the village off from access to the highway. Luckily, my Dad was there with his jeep. Somehow, he found (or carved out) a route for his vehicle and took the child to another primary health centre some twenty-three kilometres away where a doctor and nurse were able to save her life.

The child's name was Kishori. She grew attached to Dad during subsequent visits he made to the area. She was very intelligent, Dad noticed, and curious to learn about the world. Comparing notes with her father, Dad was pleased to find that Kunjam Pillai shared his enthusiasm about the girl's future, and was himself eager that his benefactor take his daughter away to a more civilized part of Kerala. And thus Dad brought Kishori to live with him on the farm at Kanjirappally; my mother too had been asking him for a while to find her some live-in help.

'But I didn't mean such a small child!' my mother remonstrated, when she saw Kishori.

'She'll grow up soon, won't she?' countered Dad.

Even though this was years before me, I'd heard the story several times, from Dad, as well as from Nirmala. Kishori died when I was barely ten, but there was a closeness that had developed between the young woman and my father. I remember him weeping bitterly, and my mother looking away as she gave instructions for the funeral.

∽

Dogs barking. Has someone entered the yard?

Oh, now they've stopped: but still panting and yelping excitedly. It's probably someone they know.

I stepped out and came face to face with Parveen who had just climbed the steps to the porch of our living room veranda. She embraced me, 'I'm so sorry, Agnes,' she said, and then as though needing to explain, 'about Pius, I mean…I'm so sorry.'

I remained stiffly unresponsive, and said rather nastily, 'Well, now look who's back from the dead….'

'What?!' asked Parveen, startled. 'Ah, you're being sarcastic. I don't blame you.... If only you knew what troubles I've seen....'

Her face was drawn and there were dark circles around her eyes.

'What's up, babe?' I embraced her again, curious and a little concerned as well.

'My sons! Rumi and Jamsheed...' and she couldn't hold back her tears anymore. Presently, she was sobbing hysterically and I was holding her in my arms, trying to console her. 'They're gone...!'

'Gone where?'

I urged her be calm and tell me what had happened.

'They had joined a pilgrimage to Najaf and Karbala.'

'Where?'

'In Iraq. Shia Muslims have their holiest shrines there. We are Sunni, as you know. We should have suspected something was not quite right—my husband and I. But the boys said it was an educational-cum-religious tour and there were many college-mates, students from their own college, who would be going along....'

'Well?'

'Apparently, once they had completed a whirlwind tour of the shrines, they dropped out of the expedition. Rumi phoned and asked me to read a note he had left for me in his drawer, in an envelope. They had planned it all well before leaving home. That's what shocks me.'

'What did their note say?'

'It said they were on their way to Syria to fight alongside the Islamic State for the new Caliphate!'

'Oh my God,' I whispered under my breath, sorry for my friend, but secretly impressed, nonetheless.

'I still hear their voices at dead of night…I imagine they're back home after a late night party! It's crazy! My babies! I still can't believe they've gone off to fight a holy war. To become martyrs. See you in Paradise, Mama. That's how their note ends.'

And once again, Parveen capsized in a sea of sobbing.

Well, children grow up so much faster than mothers imagine they do. Didn't I know that myself? Of course, in the light of her distress I didn't attempt—or quite forgot to, in fact—raise that question about Pius's past that had continued to nag me.

7

After Amma passed away, things changed rapidly on the farm. Days and months galloped past in a sort of daze. Mark was growing up fast.

My first indication of a ferment brewing in its day-to-day functioning came early one morning shortly after Pius had left for the parish office.

An unusual visitor was waiting to importune me in the antechamber of our living room: Parvati said she had tried her best to get rid of him, but the man seized her hand, pressed it to his forehead and wetting it with tears begged an audience with 'Ammachi'. It was Thomachen, an old retainer from Dad's time.

I was feeding my son in the bedroom when he arrived; past that initial famished phase when he appeared intent on swallowing an entire breast, masticating nipple and all, Mark had now settled into a ruminative sipping which indicated the onset of sleep. I could tell Thomachen wouldn't have long to wait.

∽

I recognized the old man immediately, of course, from long ago.

Always around Dad a great deal in earlier days, he had served for many years as a sort of manager, or bailiff on the plantation.

Oddly enough, once Dad was gone—and that was surely a

phase during which Amma would have needed Thomachen much more—my memory of his presence seemed to diffuse and then it wasn't there at all.

Oddly enough, only two days ago Pius had mentioned Thomas to me, saying the old man was on the prowl, probably seeking re-employment on the plantation.

'I don't trust him fully,' Pius had said. 'I'm pretty sure he was taking kickbacks from spice merchants while he was still working for your dad. He may come to see you when I'm out. Be wary of him, Mary dear....'

He shot up from the divan as soon as I entered, then stooped again and clutched my feet. I let that pass and asked him to be seated.

Sneaking but a few broken sentences through sniffles and sobs, jaw trembling uncontrollably, the old man mumbled, 'Forgive me, madam...please forgive...never thought such day coming.... Joining my hands to ask forgiveness from Chacko and Rosie's daughter....'

'But what's wrong, Thomachen? Why have you come to me? You know very well Pastor is in charge now,' I said, introducing a note of severity in my voice.

My own attention was slightly divided between trying to understand this improbable visitor's whining, and an instinctive urge to stay alert to muffled cries from the bedroom. Generally, after a good feed my son never woke up, but today I knew from his breathing his chest was congested.

'What to tell, Ammachi, how to tell all what's happened...?'

I could not bring myself to be downright rude to the old man, and asked Parvati to make him some coffee.

'So much family problem, Ammachi, how to tell?.... One hour–two hour not enough for full story.... Cousin brother—my own brother—that rascal Ignatius grabbing two-acre plot of land in Parippu: building hut: I am filing police complaint…finding good lawyer. Fixing date with magistrate, ah, but case still pending in small causes court. Now two year pass. Only two year I am not here…very urgent work keeping me away…. But I knowing this your time of need also, I'm knowing that very well—I am not here for you in your time of need, but what I can do?'

A dreadful premonition that he was at the cusp of breaking into another round of loud sobs made me raise my voice:

'But WHAT? Get on with what you came to say, Thomachen!'

Indeed, Thomas was rattled. He shuddered for an instant, stared glassily at me, then drained his cup of coffee before turning to me again.

'Your husband….'

So that sudden yell, unwarranted as it may have seemed, did have some effect in drawing him out.

'Yes? What about him?'

'Very good man…man of God…. Never I will say one word against man of God, Ammachi, never—'

'What has my husband done to you, for heaven's sake, Thomachen? Speak!'

'Pastor saying no place for me now…just think, Amma…. No place for me? No place? On Daeva Danam? Years of devoted service, now loyal retainer simply becoming pariah dog? Chacko sir never talking that way to me…Chacko sir, my best friend. Every night before sleep I still praying for his soul…. '

'Did Pastor really say that? But let's be fair, Thomachen. You have been away a long time, haven't you? You went without telling us, without notice or warning. Now, as I said, Pastor is in charge. He'll do what's best for all of us, I'm sure.'

'Begging pardon, sister, but best for who? Fifty years I am tied

The Prospect of Miracles

body and soul to Daeva Danam, to my dear Chacko sir. Seventy-two my age now.... But Pastor bringing in new contractors, all new crooks, contractors 'pitting poison on Thomachen. Most of all, Pastor not angry with me for taking long leave, swear to God, no.... Two months ago, I am arriving Daeva Danam very late one night. Bus breaking down, all garage close. Two o'clock night reaching! That making Pastor more angry! Why you coming here at this time of night? Shouting! I seeing him with Nirmala; Pastor more and more angry. Shouting at me, get out! Out! Get out...!'

'What contractors? What poison? What are you talking about? And what's Nirmala got to do with all this?'

Thoroughly frustrated with this strange deposition which I could make neither head nor tail of, I decided I had had enough of trying to be sympathetic with Thomachen.

'Thomas, I think you better go now. Take this matter—all your problems—to Pastor, whenever you want. Only Pastor is in charge now. Understand?'

'I am going, Ammachi, I am going. Please forgive, please... too much trouble I am giving you...'

After he had left and I considered some of the things he had been going on about started to make sense. Like that bit about contractors. It was true Pius had decided to contract wholesale spice dealers on a crop-wise, annual basis to purchase and dispose of our cardamom and pepper stock. Probably, he was trying to maximize profit. I could see no harm in that, nor any reason why he should have consulted me. But what was all that about Nirmala? It had made no sense at all.

I now began to wonder...had I succeeded in creating a lifelong enemy in Thomachen? By giving him short shrift in the way I had, so discourteously? And I couldn't but regret that my only reason for behaving in that manner had been prompted by Pius's words of caution urging me not to trust the old man.... Did I trust Pius that much more than anybody else?

I suppose I did. He *was* my husband.

∽

Well, quite soon, I had reason to feel even more bewildered, more disconsolate....

Three hours after Thomachen retreated from my presence, backwards and bowing with exaggerated courtesy, he was back again.

This time in the company of Pius himself; obviously, he had followed my advice and gone to see him.

Both men seemed entirely at ease, laughing over some shared aside, as they entered my living room.

'Ah, Mary Agnes, you do remember Thomachen, I'm sure? I believe you met him just a while ago?'

I merely nodded, and said, 'Yes, of course....'

'Well, I've discussed matters over with him...and I've been thinking.... You know, Thomachen's had to face some pretty hard luck in these last two years, he must have told you. It may not be such a bad idea to accept his offer to join us again?

'Primarily I need him to keep an eye on the farm's overall upkeep, as he used to in Chacko's time. What do you think?'

'Then what about Peter...?'

'And Parvati?' he prompted me. 'Why, they would continue as they have been doing all along—looking after the spice garden, with Parvati helping around the kitchen and house.

'You see, there's so much else that always needs attending to right through the year. Draining swamps when there's excess rain, repairing boundary fencing, clearing wild gorse and brushwood.

Can't quite keep up with it all by myself.... And I'm already starting to feel the pressure of parish work, as it is.

'During peak season I'm sure Peter himself will be glad for the presence of an experienced campaigner like Thomachen to advise him on spices, and their marketing. I think you may find him of some use too....'

All this would have been perfectly reasonable had he discussed it with me first. So I could air my doubts, ask him to explain his change of heart, express my fears about how such an arrangement would work. But with Thomachen seated in the sofa across us, watching me intently, nodding and breathing hard through Pius's homily, I was nonplussed, tongue-tied, and most of all, enormously mystified.

What the hell was Pius trying to do? Neither had I endorsed nor rejected anything he had proposed, yet my silence was being construed as concurrence. As Thomachen bid Pius grateful thanks and farewell, I felt like screaming in frustration at the randomness and inexplicable smugness of what seemed like a charade that had been enacted for me.

A thought crossed my mind: does he want Thomachen here so he can keep an eye on me even while he's out? Someone to report to him if I was still conversing with myself, still behaving in *mentally unstable* ways?

But I had no intention of letting him get away with this sudden volte-face without demanding an explanation.

∽

I should have known he wouldn't allow me to confront him.

It was he, in fact, who brought the matter up, almost as soon as we were alone. But without apology or explanation: it felt rather like he was turning the tables on me!

'How do I explain this to you, Mary? Do I need to, really?'

'I think you need to say something....'

'What can I say in my defence?'

Pius's voice had turned quieter, more introspective, as though probing an unusually deep substratum of his conscience. 'That despite everything I thought I knew, or suspected Thomachen of, I did not have the heart to show the old man the door?'

'But only a while ago you managed to convince me,' I replied, 'that I should be cautious, stay wary of—"the old fox" isn't that what you said?'

'I know, I know....' pacing about the living room floor, he spoke distractedly but, for once, with some humility, 'you have every right, Mary, to feel annoyed with me. But all I can say in my own defence.... When he was pleading, begging to be taken back, I could not resist a wave of compassion that overwhelmed me. I saw before me a pathetic, broken man—whom I could either help restore to life, or further pulverize by turning a deaf ear to his appeals…and condemn, eventually, to self-destruction. I'm sorry, Mary, it's the only thing I felt I could do…give him another chance. I think you should too.'

I remained silent.

'And of course, it wasn't only about compassion. To tell you the truth, compassion *and* convenience. I was thinking of you, in part, when I made this decision. I think you'll find him a useful person to have around. We are highly understaffed at the Island of the Blessed, don't you think? In any case, I've told him he need work for only three or four hours in the morning, and he's agreed to a virtual pittance for his monthly salary. He just needs to belong somewhere, to feel he's busy doing something useful. '

Was that the very first time that it dawned on me my Pastor was an accomplished and inveterate liar?

I can't remember. It may well have been.

But more often than not, it was I who was berated by *him*: for my absent-mindedness, my 'lackadaisical' indifference, my incuriosity about life, and above all, for nagging him always, my being unappreciative of how busy he really was, with no option but to keep such odd hours of work—in other words, dismissing offhand my unspecific fears and anxieties which he didn't hesitate to describe as bordering on the pathological.

Hammered by a barrage of such reproaches, I was constantly besieged by disappointments—my own—about what I had made of life, what life had made of me; and yes, undoubtedly, about those habitual tendencies I had that had become a bugbear for my husband: daydreaming or conversing with myself, even building at times visual depictions of things I most dreaded: I had really reason to worry, I began to feel, about my unhealthy mental habits.

After a few years of living like this, I became so unsure of myself there wasn't much I could say with any certainty about my years with Pastor, or even about that more recent past, after he left us.

Although I must say, if there's anything I recall with clarity to this day, it's those first years of nursing Mark.

Breastfeeding one's only child is probably the most perfect form of intimacy there is.

Of later years, hardly anything remains, not even vestigial traces. Those 'milestones' on a child's journey to boyhood, of those I can remember nothing. How it outpaced us, time, sweeping past one at full tilt, defacing, burying so much in its tyrannical wake: all that was sullied by bewilderment, by betrayal, all that's lost…. Or is it?

After all, this account of my marriage perhaps isn't quite so garbled as it might appear at first. My experience with Pius really did unfold in exactly the way I have recorded it: confused, terrified, defensive.

Yes, emotional pain jumbles events, creating its own alleyways of evasion. Extreme jealousy engenders pain so profound it plunges one into fathomless pits of panic, obsessive depression. All unwarranted, as Pius would have had me believe? My own desperate insecurities solely responsible for driving him—and me—to despair, turning him into a defeated Job of despondency? A good man wronged by a harridan whose insane psychological fears—oh, how he loved to suggest that's all it was—were simply a fabrication of her diseased mind?

∽

On the other hand, outside the confines of our home the Pastor grew from strength to strength. I couldn't help but feel envious of his stature among parishioners, whose adulation he leeched off. But within the privacy of home, our tussle remained pitiless. I had no one to talk to.

Suddenly, Mark is all of thirteen: at least in a version of memory that clings tenaciously to me: he springs out of a corner with a sudden leap and a gruff bark. To startle me, although at thirteen? Would he still have been playing such games?

No, probably not.

∽

Considerably older than Parveen's sons Rumi and Jamsheed, Mark was indisputable leader of the gang.

Yet, in their company, an almost gentle kindliness emerged

in him towards the younger boys.

Like Parveen and me before them, they were all students at Loyola. Since its inception as a girls' boarding school thirty years ago, it had expanded into a co-ed and now also took in local day scholars. The younger fellows would certainly have had their own playmates at school, but sometimes, on a Saturday their mother brought them over to lunch, and all of them would spend the remainder of the day at Daeva Danam.

The whole afternoon then, until it grew dark, all three boys were at their happiest; it was Mark who was the organizer of games and pastimes: cricket and football always a preference, especially if it were raining, but sometimes an elaborate treasure hunt incorporating names of trees on our spice farm, with clues scribbled on chits of paper in Mark's methodical hand.

And once, during the summer holidays—he must have been fifteen or sixteen—single-handedly he adapted *King Lear* into a shorter set piece of ten or twelve scenes: then assigning roles and roping in other Loyolites from the neighbourhood made players copy out their parts, organized rehearsals, and presented an evening's entertainment for Pastor and his wife, and parents of all participating children, as well as a few of our other adult friends.

Needless to say, Mark played Lear himself, while the youngest, Jamsheed, played Cordelia (lightweight enough for his father to be able to lug her corpse tenderly in his arms during that final scene).

The performance was indeed an exceptional effort, put together over a two-month end-of-year school vacation; and despite the tremendous ovation they received for it—an ideal way it would seem to expend those lazy leisure hours—the boys never cared to repeat such a dramatic exercise.

But any other holiday, too, whether during term or on weekends, if spent at Daeva Danam was undoubtedly a treat for the boys. For Parveen as well, who got a chance to get away from domestic chores and her overbearing husband, sharing the pleasures of concocting and preparing a menu alongside me that brightened her hours and stimulated young palates.

Mark always took immense pride, of course, in being the eldest, the acknowledged wisest of the lot. Sometimes, he tried his hand at cooking, or suggested an outlandish variation to a standard recipe which, when tried out, against better counsel, was usually found to be rather effective.

Always diligent, a much-lauded student, in his final year at school, Mark turned unexpectedly disinterested and sullen.

He refused to discuss his problems with his parents, denied there *were* any.

In the past he had spoken of wanting to write stories, at times had maintained an occasional journal. Now he said he didn't see the point in becoming a 'scribe', even disavowed any serious interest in writing at all.

All he felt like doing, he said, was 'social work'!

Now this was astonishing, apart from sounding corny coming from someone so young!

Yet, it was clear that the awakening of Mark's social conscience didn't happen in a flash: its growth should have been evident to us—to me, at least—in sardonic comments and observations he had a habit of making. At times it seemed he was just trying to be witty or show off his extra-sensitive habits of observation.

But really, these should have been warning signals: they were in fact simply dribs and drabs of painful awareness that pointed to a keen acuity into the less fortunate members of our community. He hardly ever spoke about this or any other matter openly to me, and not at all to his father, of whom he remained slightly wary, perhaps even a little afraid; but he could be pretty forthright when alone with me.

Later I came to realize it wasn't his father he feared so much as the force of his own indignation about everything the Pastor stood for and preached about. After he turned fourteen, Mark could no longer be enticed to attend Pius's services or listen to his sermons. This was a drastic change from a younger period during which he'd never miss a single Sunday morning, even if he were unwell, to proudly soak in every word his father declaimed from the pulpit.

An avid reader from an early age, I began to notice Mark much absorbed in authors I was not familiar with: someone called Frantz Fanon, for instance, as well as other books by a Fr. Arturo Paoli and yet another by Fr. Gustavo Gutierrez. At Pius's own express suggestion, I had kept him regularly informed about Mark's reading habits. When I showed him these books, he exclaimed:

'Ah…! Liberation theology already? I must have a heart-to heart with my boy….'

∽

'I completely understand how you feel, son,' Pius said to him, one somnolent Sunday afternoon when lunch was over.

'The plight of the poor and dispossessed in our world is so very terrible. One should never look away from it. I agree, that would be a most unchristian thing to do.'

Looking up from the book he had only just got back to poring into, Mark eyed him uncomprehendingly.

'I'm just reading….' he muttered.

'Yes, of course. But you won't need to read further than the

Word of our Lord to understand why the world is how it is. He has His plans for everyone and everything. And if you only read the Bible, it will give you a fuller understanding of everything.'

'Really?' said Mark. 'Everyone and everything? You make the Lord sound like a super management guru.'

'Ha-ha, ha-ha,' Pius laughed appreciatively. 'He is, He is... but do tell me, what's bothering you, son? Let's talk frankly.'

'Just look around and you'll know yourself. When you say everyone and everything does that include the old thotti who comes to our back door every morning?'

'What old thotti? That's not a nice word to use, Mark. Thottis were manual scavengers. I don't believe there are any more people engaged in this work. Except perhaps—not likely even in the remotest villages. What you mean is the municipal sweeper who comes to take away the garbage?'

'Ah, so you do see how it is, Dad? The kind of work the old man does seven days a week—call him what you will—isn't very nice either. It's what makes him in the eyes of society untouchable.

'And after cleaning our shit-pots, he sweeps the entire yard. Do you mean he doesn't deserve any better than the four hundred rupees we pay him every month for his services—because that's God's particular plan for him?'

'Everything in the world happens as God deems fit, son. We have to pray for the grace to understand His intent, show reverence for His Grand Design. Do you think there's anything even remotely random about the movement of the planets, the stars you see in the night sky?

'Not an inch, not a fraction of a second is variable in the wondrous infinity of His immeasurable Creation. You've learnt all this in your science class at school, I'm sure: the clockwork precision of it all.'

The Prospect of Miracles

I was concealed in a small alcove outside Mark's study room listening to every word of their conversation. I hadn't meant to eavesdrop, but nor did I want to miss any of it.

'If we can accept the sense and proportion of His Creation up there,' here he pointed a finger heavenward, 'why do we find it so difficult to accept His plans for us, down here, closer to Earth? Can we blame Him if our impatience prevents comprehension of why things are the way they are down here?'

Mark didn't answer.

'If you want to be a writer, I should tell you....' Pius continued.

'Oh, I'm not even sure I want to any more.'

'Ah, perseverance is no mean virtue, son. You shouldn't give up without trying hard enough. But what I want to say is: you can be the greatest writer in the world if you want to,' said Pius encouragingly. 'If only you seek to imitate our Lord Jesus Christ....'

I couldn't see either Mark or Pius from where I stood, nor could they see me, but I was imagining Mark's expression from his the tone of his responses; nor was I able to really guess what Pius was leading up to. But in that instant, I felt him sit up: Pius had indeed succeeded in grabbing his son's attention.

'In what way do you mean, Dad?'

'Well, He was the greatest Romantic poet ever, wouldn't you say? It was His great imagination that allowed Him to feel for and heal lepers, the lame, the blind, to heal the multitudes of ailing peasants who came to Him for succour.... To raise Lazarus from the dead even four days after he became a corpse! Yes, the Great Imaginator, but also the Son of God who could make real that which He dreamed of. Isn't that the best gift a writer could have?'

'Hmm,' was all Mark was willing to aspirate by way of response.

'Pray to the Lord for that gift of great imagination. Then see how well you start writing.'

No reply.

'Everything else will go well, too. Your schoolwork, your exams, your college admissions. For a start, Mark, why not try attending Sunday service again?'

'I knew there was a catch somewhere....'

Again, I wasn't looking at them but in Mark's tone of voice I detected a wry exchange of amusement. His father, too, was probably grinning widely at him. Perhaps by way of conciliation, I heard Mark mutter, 'Maybe I will....'

'Thank you, son, I thank you....'

But there must have been a deeper sense of betrayal that they hadn't touched upon. Pius was speaking all too soon when he alluded to college admissions! At the time I speak of, Mark was still in his final year at school, perhaps not yet fully aware of the disquieting aspects of his parents' personal life—I wasn't myself—or perhaps he was only reacting to something he had sensed of Pius's prickly hypocrisy at an entirely subconscious level.

In any case, Mark never did attend a single one of Pius's services again; nor, for that matter, did he enrol at any college. He quietly dropped out of school, and left home—I mean ran away. For days he was only an entry in the missing persons' file of the police, and I, although probably aware in my heart of hearts that he was alive and unhurt, insane with grief and anxiety.

A few weeks later he wrote to us from Delhi. He was staying with someone he had first met while still at school, but a few years his senior; an older boy called Nelson Kuruvilla who had relocated himself to the capital. This Nelson, like Mark, was also preoccupied with 'social work', you could say, in fact, as we came to learn much later, he was an important functionary in the country's political underground—what in our country the government and its police describe as 'Naxalites'.

If I am not mistaken that was the very year in which the first of the Kottayam riots rattled Kerala and wreaked destruction in our languid town of Kanjirappally. Our church, among other properties, was ransacked by hooligans belonging to a right-wing political formation, the altar set on fire.

Although momentarily I felt glad that Mark was safe a thousand miles away, I do remember an irrational notion that crossed my mind at the time: that these violent disturbances mirrored Mark's own disgust with Pius and all the ideas he had tried to impress on him.

8

When Mark decided to remit himself from his parents' lives, was it sheer disgust that prompted flight?

Yet what could he have witnessed, overheard or imagined that made him run away? I still can't guess. Because only after he made his escape, all the acrimony and deceit festering deep in our submerged and duplicitous worlds floated to the surface, like so much scum: no sudden detonations or apocalyptic showdowns: only a series of low, excruciating rumbles impending disaster.

In the beginning Pius chose to pretend that my misapprehensions about his private life could entirely be attributed to my own emotional insecurities. My perceiving it as a secret 'double life' he was leading was simply a 'temperamental flaw' in my mental make-up; he described this 'aberration' in colourful phrases as a 'psychological mistrust of loved ones', or 'predilection for doubting' and possibly even a 'disturbed line of heredity' that he traced back to my dad, incredibly claiming that Chacko had for years maintained a resident mistress in Kishori, Nirmala's mother—the tribal girl he had 'rescued' from Attappady—further insinuating that Rosalie knew all about their liaison but had decided to look the other way.

So, according to Pius, my childhood would surely have been clouded by a subconscious awareness of murky, camouflaged goings-on which offered, according to him, the most plausible explanation for my persistent fears, my unabated sense of vulnerability.

How the hell did he find out all this—about my dad, I mean? I should have challenged him right then but didn't see the point in trying to pin him down, and later having to sift straws of purported reality from conjecture and lie.

Kishori, at the time he was referring to, couldn't have been more than half my father's age!

And yet, I had to admit there was a ring of truth to his claim: I tried hard to recollect any childhood memories to corroborate it, but came up with only a vague sense of unease, half-remembered quarrels between my parents eavesdropped on. And most of all, the unforgettable spectacle of my father on his knees, weeping bitterly like a child before the supine figure of Kishori lifeless on the floor of her hut.

The fact is bonded labour wasn't uncommon on feudal Nazrani plantations until just a few years ago, and even now, one continues to hear stories of landlords reaping the exploitative pleasures of such entrenched social contract. But what angered me more than anything else about Pius's diatribe against Chacko was that he brought up some of Dad's peculiar idiosyncrasies—such as his habit, while walking his gorgeously long-haired Alsatian bitch, Sylvie, of engaging in extended conversations in Malayalam, or his other unique habit of gesticulating theatrically to himself when strolling quite alone through the shady plantation pathways, as though deep in converse with an absent colleague.

Which, in the end, my husband couldn't help connect to his chief disconsolation, blaming my nervous anguish on what he called 'flirting with insanity': my deliberate and dangerous disregard of his well-meant warning not to indulge in conversations with myself!

I didn't myself believe this for a moment, but refused to say anything in my own defence. Mostly, I was shocked speechless that he had no compunctions about raking up family history for clues of suppressed insanity which, by implication, had trickled down to me! I hated him for this, as for all the insidious tricks he began to play on me from then on.

∽

Soon a deadly game of cat and mouse began between Pius and me.

Watching all the time—or so I felt—quick to pounce on any lapse of memory or judgement on my part as if seeking the slightest opportunity to establish my incompetence, faulty judgement or sloppy living habits—all of which, according to him, I had successfully imparted to my son. These skirmishes of discord and disagreement, if overheard by Mark while he was still living with us, would certainly have been permanently branded in his consciousness, or so I imagined—something I could never forgive Pius for. But that was the least of it.

There were other times when I felt he was deviously and mischievously trying to show me up as being an unfocused dreamer who didn't have an entirely firm grasp on reality; that I was probably quite delusional, besides being hysterical and paranoid.

His brazen manipulation of my feelings amazes me to this day! Although during the time I was subjected to it, it caused much anxiety and self-doubt. I crumpled, almost prepared to go down on my knees and plead insanity—anything for some peace.

Our austere prayer hut, always spotlessly clean, had but one small wooden table in it by way of furniture. On it stood a bronze crucifix.

It was a place of retreat for Pius. Before leaving the house every morning, and often in the evening too, he would spend quiet moments alone with himself—and his God, I presume. What came over me one morning I cannot say, but on impulse I placed at the foot of the crucifix, a bunch of freshly-cut champak flowers from our nursery.

He had had a late start that day, and some appointment to meet as well. I happened to be seeing him off when we entered the prayer room together that morning. He turned pale, and momentarily froze.

'They're fresh.... I cut them just now....'

Flustered, defensive was how I felt; but he replied with measured softness:

'I don't doubt that, Mary Agnes....' his voice was cold as ice, dripping with kindness and hauteur.

'Please clean up this—mess, Agnes, as soon as I leave. And do remember, dear, our Lord doesn't expect us to pander Him with unchaste offerings.'

Unchaste offerings? Flowers? But I knew better than to argue.

As he walked away without any leave-taking or the slightest gesture of farewell, I heard in my head the sharp riposte he might have made to any commonsensical objection I might have raised: Hindus use flowers in their rituals, for God's sake. Not us!

No, I would never have dreamt of deliberately ignoring or opposing his wishes. But the next day, when he came home at lunchtime, he went straight to the prayer room again.

In itself, nothing so unusual about this: as I said, he often sought a few minutes to himself whenever he got home, or before stepping out. Yet what ensued a moment or so later was extraordinary in the extreme.

I heard sounds, noises, grunts of disapproval and despair. Instinctively, I knew they were directed at me—there was no one else around—my stomach churned, shrivelled in unthinking fear.

The thought occurred then, for the first time, perhaps irrationally: Pius doesn't love me anymore, perhaps never did. His constant coldness and cruelty had begun to grate, unnerving as well as bewildering me. But it took me a long time to mentally accept this new formulation which I wasn't even convinced was true: I didn't allow myself to believe it. And there was always the possibility that this entire disturbance in my life was simply based on some misunderstanding, some absence of clarification, such as usually results from faulty communication.

'Agnes…! Mary Agnes!'

Was he yelling out for me?

'Come here, Agnes!'

Yes, he had raised his voice; he was shouting!

'Just a minute, Pius….'

It took me no more than a few seconds to rush to the prayer room. But there, at its threshold I faltered, my mouth falling open. Pius was standing by the altar. On the floor, in front of it were scattered a whole array of champak flowers; such as I had placed there the previous day, only many more.

'I thought I told you. Why only yesterday we discussed this in a civilized manner. I told you quite clearly—'

'But…but…I don't remember—' I stood there, stuttering. 'I threw them out first thing you left. That was yesterday morning. I threw them on the garbage heap in the backyard.'

I found myself stooping, collecting the scattered champak blossoms from the floor. He had flung them so angrily they had spread to every corner of the room.

'Parvati burned them along with the other rubbish…. That was yesterday.' I repeated breathlessly, continuing to collect the flowers, apologizing, as if I had indeed been responsible for them.

'Then someone else, no doubt, has been inspired to emulate your example. I found this bunch on the altar just now.... A minute ago. The flowers definitely look quite fresh to me.'

'No, no. That's impossible. There is no one else here! No one's been to the prayer room since you went out. Who on earth could possibly have done this?'

'Well then, the obvious answer to that—ask yourself: could it be you, following your own impulses mindlessly?' he stared querulously at me, a look of pathetic self-pity on his face. 'Then forgetting who's responsible? Oh, Mary, what's come over you? Why's all this happening to us, I ask you?'

'All what? I didn't, Pius, I'm sorry but I don't know what you are talking about. I know I didn't put any flowers on the altar again, not today. Not a second time! I'm not quite so mad!'

'Then what is it after all you are sorry about, Mary Agnes?' he said, with a hint of amusement at my anguish.

I said nothing in reply, and he turned away with a look of contempt.

Although I knew the truth about what I had or hadn't done, just for that one moment I felt utterly confused, and began to cry. Could it be? Had I done this? Could I actually have forgotten?

'I swear I didn't! I didn't put any flowers there!'

I insisted once more, shouting after his receding figure.

To register his protest or his disgust, he left the farmhouse and went out again without eating any lunch.

I could see he hadn't cared to listen, or debate the issue with me; what was more, he had made it clear by his manner that he was terribly disappointed—I was, too—especially in that I had raised my voice at him.

By now alone, my tears were flowing copiously. They were tears of frustration that my avowal hadn't been sufficient to convince Pius; he continued to doubt my word!

And only so many minutes later, after they had dried and he had gone out again, I did allow myself a measure of self-examination. I tried to think back calmly on the events of that day. What had I done since morning? I remembered making myself a bowl of hot oats porridge and, after eating it, wandering through the meandering garden paths. I had in fact—I remembered this quite vividly—stopped by the nursery, admired the pale brick-red roses that had come up so well and the bush of purple asters, even stooped and whispered a loving word of encouragement to my gladioli…but champak blossoms? I had no memory at all of observing them, let alone of having collected a bunch!

After I had been alone with myself for a while, I posed yet another question to myself: if I hadn't put those flowers on the altar, there was only one other person who could have—only Pius could have planted the flowers there himself when he came back at lunchtime.

Deliberately. What's he trying to do? Frighten me? Make me feel insane? If that was true, wasn't that a horrid thing to do to your own wife?

And then suddenly I felt submerged in the bleakest of depressions.

∽

He came back home later that afternoon, and asked very politely if I could make him a cup of tea.

'I slept badly last night, and woke up with a headache,' he explained, '—which hasn't entirely cleared up yet.'

'Oh, poor you,' I said, not intending sarcasm at all, as I hastened to the kitchen to boil some water for his tea. I was actually relieved to find he was speaking to me in a normal tone of voice, as though the distressing exchange of words a few hours earlier had never taken place.

After drinking his cup of tea, he went in to rest for a while.

Sometimes, early evening, while it was still light, he would eat his supper and go out again. Was he planning to go out this evening too, I asked him?

'*You* needn't stay up, please,' he instructed me firmly. 'Try to get a good night's sleep, darling.'

On most occasions he was very kind to me, as he was to everyone else. But sometimes, I just couldn't help disobey. About sleeping so early it was often like that—I found it impossible. I'd wait and wait for him until I dozed off, overwhelmed.

Once, I opened my eyes after having dropped off for a while and gazed uncomprehendingly at the wall clock. Ten minutes to two? Was Pius not back yet? I was alarmed, worried.

Then I saw him: posing in front of the bedroom mirror, examining his own reflection intently, with an air of obvious self-satisfaction.

'Pius....'

He was fully dressed. My voice, hoarse with sleep, startled him.

'Go back to sleep,' he said in a hushed undertone.

'But why so late?' I asked him.

'Parish work...shh. Don't disturb your sleep,' he muttered something else inaudibly, and began to change into his nightclothes.

Frankly, that was not the first time I felt utter disbelief about this claim. What parish work goes on till two in the morning? And there would surely have been other nights when I hadn't woken up, hadn't confronted him.

But I held my silence.

9

At the edge of the field, not far from the tribal women's huts, was a tiny disused cottage under a jackfruit tree whose foliage had flourished so impressively that on the sunniest of mornings its vast green canopy admitted only hints of speckled light.

One more outhouse or storeroom in which Amma had, at some point in the past put away various knick-knacks, unwanted household furniture, kitchenware of uncertain functional value, old sticks of lumber, clusters of worthless oddments; nonetheless, so much of it had been clearly difficult to get rid of: a bronze horse about two-feet-tall with a rider, another without, a huge copper vat with a built-in under-brazier for heating bathwater, a wooden chest of drawers entirely coated in mould, various curiously shaped pots, pans, clay gourds, cooking vessels, sooty figurines of men and women engaged in dance, dalliance or playing musical instruments; all in various stages of neglect and ruination.

I wouldn't myself have described it as 'a whole lot of junk', but those were Pius's words as he grumbled about Amma's inability to jettison the unwanted and unusable, while Peter and Parvati cleaned and swept out the shed. Once there was enough room inside, he had a desk, a chair and a cot moved in. By the end of the morning the cottage had taken on quite a pleasant aspect.

This was to be his study, he said: the servants, myself and even Mark (little more than a toddler, who would never have dared to wander to a remote edge of the garden after dark) were all instructed in no uncertain terms that he was never to be disturbed here.

But a certain amount of ambiguity, if not mystery, remained as to what this work was that he would be engaged in, and when. Only at night it would seem, after Mark and I had been bundled off to bed?

What was he so busy doing? Reading, perhaps? Making notes for his Sunday sermon? And if he was really working here, why did he prefer to use such a low wattage bulb to create a dark, cavernous workspace? Were his eyes giving him trouble?

Once or twice, after my son had fallen asleep I did venture out for a short stroll into the balmy night and saw, beyond the tangle of pepper vines and clumps of cardamom trees, a single light glowing faintly in the distance.

Yes, Pius was at work in his study.

In the end, it was a difficult question I had to answer for myself. I pondered and puzzled over it for days and weeks: Is it possible for a man to harbour spiritual aspirations, and yet be powerless against lascivious impulses?

Evidently, yes. But this perverse truth became intelligible to me in a most painfully convoluted fashion.

What were the first signs that aroused suspicion? Strange smells perhaps, a glow or a shadow darkening his visage every time he returned to our bedroom in the small hours? As with most things, I don't recall specific details.

But one thing I should mention: Pius was very vain, a real dandy. He took hours preening himself, combing his hair; then, just before stepping out he'd run a hand lightly through his carefully arranged hairdo so as to just slightly disarrange it! I have to admit, my parents had a point when they had warned me I didn't know him well enough.

But before he was willing to admit his own culpability in the matter—he never really did—I had to face a gruelling barrage of accusations:

'Insecure, jealous woman! Hysterical harpy I should call you…that's the creature I married!'

These were but a few of the most graphic epithets his retaliatory onslaughts comprised of.

In my desperation to unearth what ailed our marriage, I suppose I did seek answers from him rather relentlessly, which bugged him no end. Although, I must confess, there's one unforgettable scene that refuses to go away, horribly impressed in memory, which makes me wonder even today if I had not in fact got him completely wrong, and should have apologized for my suspicious behaviour?

'What do you want me to do?' he screamed at me once, angry and agitated. 'Fall at your feet and implore there is no other woman in my life? Bang my head against the wall till it bleeds? Just to prove how frustrating you can be, woman!'

For a few seconds he was silent, taking deep breaths to calm himself; then he apologized.

'I'm sorry…I'm sorry, Agnes. I got carried away. I should show more patience when these obsessive fears take hold of you. Please forgive me, Mary….'

But equally, there's another scene that yet haunts me. I can never forget how terrified I was of him.

Some instinct had prompted me to take a walk one night in the direction of Pius's workroom. It was a dark night and the wind was high in the trees, thrashing and howling. Rain was about to start pouring. But for some reason I continued to walk towards his low-lit workroom. In all that tumult of natural elements I don't know how he could have heard my footsteps on the gravel, but he did.

'Who's there?!'

His sharp voice rang through the night and I froze in fear where I stood, just a few feet from his hut.

'Yes? Is that you, Agnes?'

Suddenly, he flung the door open and stood there under the lighted doorway, his face grimacing with anger. I was standing in darkness outside, but I could feel his gaze directed straight at me.

'Yes?' he repeated, demanding an answer. 'What do you want, Mary Agnes? Is it too much to ask for a little privacy while I work?'

'I didn't mean to disturb you, Pius…I'm sorry. I thought I heard voices—'

'Voices! Ah, but those you've been hearing in your head ever since I've known you. Will it satisfy you to come in and check that there's nobody hiding in here with me? Come, come in, please, and satisfy yourself.'

If he were bluffing when he made that invitation, he certainly succeeded in brushing me off course any further probing. After that outburst, I didn't dare move an inch closer to his hut, simply turned and headed straight back to our living quarters, continuing to mutter apologies,

'I'm sorry, I'm so sorry Pius…. Please try to get back to your work….'

Despite the chill in the air, when I got home I noticed my shirt was damp, I was in a cold sweat and had to change. And then suddenly I remembered something else—could I have imagined it? A mere olfactory hint, on a windy evening—can't be absolutely certain—but wasn't that a whiff of alcohol I got when he opened the door and stood glaring at me?

II

THE FOREST OF ATTAPPADY

10

(i)

As a child, Nirmala had often slept poorly.

Some nights she woke up feeling famished and found herself alone—her mother not in bed beside her, where she should have been.

Occasionally, these unexplained absences roused her to fits of intense rage.

She sat up and howled, shrieking for her Amma. Often enough, though, enfeebled by sleep, and with no promise of respite from hunger pangs, she slid back into fitful slumber.

One evening, Kishori explained to Nirmala before putting her to bed that she must understand Amma's duties never ended; not until both master and mistress were fast asleep. Sometimes mudalali summoned her to his room at night—and then she had to attend to him. It was all part of her duties.

'Once you fall asleep, never wake up until it's light again—even if I'm not here beside you. That's why the landlord lets us live on his farm; it's all part of the job I do for him. And when you grow up, perhaps…if we are still here, God willing, it may become a part of yours, too.'

(ii)

By no means were these her mother's last words to her.

But reaffirmed and repeated several times over the years—and towards the end, too, in that month of fever and convulsion that tossed her mother into a storm of delirious raving and eventually, on that irreversible journey from which none returns—Nirmala had just turned fourteen.

When she realized her mother was dead, those words rang in her ears before all others—Kishori making that strange portent—or was it forewarning?

Drained of all emotion by his outrageous display of grief for Kishori—Amma Rosalie embarrassed by its histrionic clamour, what would the servants think?—Chacko remained abstracted for weeks on end in a world of his own: thus extending to Nirmala a grace period in which to continue being a child.

Later—although only once—the mudalali did call her to his side:

'Come closer, mol....'

He put his arms around her and kissed her forehead, ruffling her hair affectionately: Nirmala froze, almost choking, unable to breathe. Disquieting as this gesture was to a teenager not yet fifteen, Nirmala had no notion what to make of it, yet she was frightened. Presently, the landlord released her from his embrace.

To himself he justified his now diminished throb of craving as an inability to get over the love of his life, Kishori. But probably this just wasn't true. And any other explanation, such as that with advancing age impotence loomed closer than ever he just wasn't willing to consider.

Moreover, by this time, fresh troubles had descended on

Chacko's broad shoulders, new unexpected ones that roused him from his solipsistic detachment.

(iii)

A young man was often on the plantation in those days, some sort of electrical contractor who was often assigned odd jobs at Daeva Danam.

The landlord found his mannerisms amusingly ostentatious, although friendly, and made fun of him after he left—ensuring however, if he did, that Mary Agnes wasn't within earshot. The landlord's daughter seemed to have hit it off rather well with this young man.

One day Chacko sir asked this contractor—his name was Pascal—to install a tube-light in Nirmala's shack.

Pascal came into the hut early one morning to enquire of her, now its lone occupant, which she thought the ideal position would be; and then, after measuring the distance to the closest electrical junction-box with a tractable tape-roll he proceeded to the market to make purchases.

When he returned he was carrying a long projectile wrapped in newspaper, presumably the fluorescent tube itself, and a small satchel of wires, screws and tools. By now it was already late evening.

He commenced installing the tube-light, but soon had to ask Nirmala to light the petromax for him. He assured her it wouldn't take him long to complete the work.

Two hours later, he was still at it. Now at least the tube was fixed, but there was no power supply for him to check if it worked.

Both electrician and girl were feeling rather hungry. They turned their attention to a packet of crispy snacks that Pascal had remembered to buy in the market. Nirmala provided a plastic plate to serve them in. The fried savoury crunchies were totally cold, of course, but no less delicious. The young man and the not-so-young girl ate their fill.

'Anyway,' said Pascal, after they had wiped it all up, 'that took care of my dinner. Are you still hungry?'

Nirmala shook her head.

'In a few minutes the power will be back, and a nice bright light will flood your room. So do enjoy these last moments of a charming yellow glow,' he said, indicating the petromax.

Sitting beside her on the cold hard floor in semi-darkness, the electrician made Nirmala feel relaxed, asking her thoughtful question after question about village life in her native place. Did she miss it? Would she ever go back there now that her mother was no more?

He spoke in a low, reassuring voice, as though the darkness outside rendered him more sympathetic, muffling his words to a whisper.

Two or three times he got up to turn on the newly installed switch by the hut's entrance hoping the tube-light would blink and flash on brightly. But no, it didn't.

'We'll just leave it on, I guess,' he said. 'I want to be sure it's not me that's tripped up or made some blunder in the wiring....'

But it was evident there were no lights anywhere on the plantation; although it was a clear night, with an almost full moon and many bright stars in the sky.

'What will you do in the dark, if the power doesn't come back all night?'

'I'm not afraid,' said Nirmala, secretly thinking, I'll just go to bed as soon as you leave.

'No, of course, you're not,' said Pascal. 'You're grown up now...and a beautiful young woman, too. Well, let's not worry about the light too much. Maybe we could have some tea while we wait?

'There's no milk.'

'Black is fine. And after, maybe just put that thing off, will you? Don't waste your kerosene....'

Animated and made more wakeful by the tea, Pascal kept up his friendly chatter, unmindful of the late hour. Presently, he ran his nails lightly over the young girl's bare arm, while giggling pleasurably to himself.

Nirmala recoiled at his touch with an expression of disgust. 'Stturh...!'

Annoyance, surprise, disapproval? But such a tame rebuff did little to dampen Pascal's brazen laughter, or restrain his gentle caresses on her dark soft flesh. Nirmala was about to get up and move away. Just then Pascal stroked her arm one more time, so lovingly—his face close to hers, whispering something in her ear: she couldn't quite hear what he had mumbled, but the touch of his soft lips against her ear sent a shudder coursing through her body. The momentary, unfamiliar thrill surprised and disconcerted her. Could he have noticed to what extent his touch had electrified her? She hoped not.

But no, unmindful of the effects of his seductive onslaught, Pascal had resumed a unilateral jubilation, giggling louder than before, tickling her arm even more unabashedly. Not knowing how to react, Nirmala made embarrassed noises of discontent, and finally settled for a chortle of half-hearted protest.

Emboldened by what he perceived as encouragement, Pascal suggested rather assertively now that there was no sense in wasting kerosene, they just didn't need the petromax on.

'It's a crime to waste natural resources,' he said. 'Soon there'll be no kerosene left in the whole wide world! You won't be able to purchase it for love or money! I promise you I'm not going anywhere, not until that damn tube-light flickers to life. Don't be afraid...I promise,' he reassured Nirmala. 'We can sit here in the dark without fear of anyone or anything....'

'But I want to sleep now,' she complained in a soft voice. 'It's so late!'

'Ah, don't tell me you're sleepy already, Nirmala.... You're big woman now, not a baby!'

The electricity didn't come back until the small hours, and Pascal just wasn't prepared to leave. Finally, with the petromax extinguished—he had absolutely insisted on that—he proceeded under cover of darkness to initiate Nirmala into forms of tactile pleasure she had never before experienced, which gave her great joy yet frightened her terribly, leaving her with a sorrowful sense of depletion that made her weep. He wiped her tears and soothed her sobs, saying she had nothing to feel bad about: what they had done together only made them friends forever—and she needed a true friend like him, especially now that her mother was no more.

(iv)

For months after that night, the contractor didn't come back to her shack to see her. Nirmala was understandably hurt by this show of indifference.

She waited, looking out for him eagerly every day; but there was no sign of Pascal.

Once, she saw him walking in the distance behind the mudalali. He saw her too—she was quite sure of that—but didn't wave, or acknowledge her presence; maybe he didn't want the landlord to know they were friends?

Another time, she saw him driving a battered, old SUV with

Chechi beside him in the front seat.

Then unexpectedly, thanks to Parvati—who never could resist gossip—Nirmala was privy to news of all the fuss and excitement and anger that had erupted on the estate without her slightest knowledge; and learned the dreadful cause of the tumult: Chechi, and the man called Pascal were to be wed. And what was more, as a result they would not be living on the farm anymore!

They were moving to a place some miles away called Kumily where they had rented a cottage. Behind this break-up of the peaceful spice-growing family there was no precipitating cause other than the landlord's implacable rage—he had sworn never to condone them—not just the marriage they were entering into in cussed opposition to her parents' wishes—but yet another outrageous decision the couple had arbitrarily committed to.

Apparently, only recently, Pascal the electrician had thrown his lot in with a group of Protestant evangelists called Assembly of Heaven's Elect. Chechi's wedding would take place next week at a Protestant church in Kottayam. What's more, Pascal, her husband-to-be, had not only decided to forsake the Nazrani tradition he had been born into but had enrolled for training as a pastor with this relatively new church. To lend further flourish to his now transformed identity, he had solemnly decided to add a prefix to his name: from now on he would be known as Pius Pascal Philipose.

'Such a joke!' Chacko was enraged and indignant, 'is it self-delusion or public deception? Does he really think everyone will believe he's pious just because he calls himself that? Didn't I tell you he has the makings of a charlatan, Mary Agnes? And you actually want to live with someone who calls himself pious?'

'I do, Appa,' said Agnes, trying to remain calm. 'I know he loves me. Besides, he takes the name after his great-grandfather to whom he was apparently very close as a child. That's why the name means so much to him. And as for evangelism, he really does believe, and wants to devote his life to spreading the word of Christ Jesus.'

Despite the sense of peace that prevailed in normal times on Daeva Danam, whose large overgrown spaces generally subsumed all else, great, rancorous scenes would surely have echoed through its inner lived-in rooms—Nirmala might have derived some perverse satisfaction had she overheard cries of ridicule and rage against the forthcoming wedding—but in reality, no such voices came to her ears and she had to be content with purported hearsay: only surmise and fanciful conjecture from Parvati about the distress in the lives of the landlord's family—during those three days when Agnes, with the help of her pastor-in-training, packed her things and moved out.

Only Amma Rosalie and a dazed but distinctly resentful Nirmala—in a floral sequinned sari and blouse, 'specially stitched to size by the family tailor'—were present at Mary Agnes's wedding. Chacko stayed away to register his protest and unqualified disapproval.

(v)

The dream of love that had overwhelmed Nirmala on that electric evening while she waited with Pascal for her tube-light to activate, was, alas, no more than a dream: deep down she already knew that.

An unendurably painful awareness seeped in—that Pascal had merely seized the moment of their togetherness so late at night to pretend affection, stimulate, and then enjoy her physically.

That in doing so he had enabled her to discover something pleasurable beyond imagining about her own body was entirely secondary to the great joy and hope Nirmala had felt in the promise of sustained intimacy and friendship. But all that, she reluctantly admitted to herself now, had been no more than make-believe—an illusion contrived by her own mind—as fleeting as a cloud street on a radiantly starry night.

But neither weary resignation, nor the powerful lassitude that engulfed her could subdue an imp of resentment that took birth within Nirmala in that moment. She didn't nurture or feed him; yet every now and then—when she had quite forgotten his existence—he would raise his tiny head and ululate his grief.

Just a few days after the reception she had attended in the company of Amma Rosalie, unexpectedly, she requested leave of absence. She claimed she had received a phone call just that morning from an uncle—or did she say cousin?—in Attappady. She simply had to visit her aunt immediately—Kishori's younger sister—who was very ill and dying.

(vi)

For a while Nirmala, who had not undertaken this long journey in years, and never except in the company of her mother, was amazed at how simple and comfortable it was in comparison to the impression she had retained from so many years ago. Perhaps things had improved that much, with so many more buses and all the progress consecutive governments had made.

Amma Rosalie had generously given her twelve hundred rupees in small notes before she set out from Daeva Danam to cover her travel expense. That seemed a great amount to Nirmala who thanked her profusely but secretly hoped to use it so sparingly that when she got back to the farm she might still have some part of it left. Once she reached her village, Edavani, of course, her relations and other tribal folk wouldn't allow her to spend anything, she assumed; and what was there to spend on anyway in the forest?

From Kanjirappally she had caught a local bus to the main depot at Kottayam. Here, another Kerala Transport bus was waiting to depart for Thrissur. She would have missed it while waiting in queue to ask directions were it not for an elderly traveller who had casually enquired about her destination, and urged her to jump onto a bus about to depart.

At Thrissur she had a long wait of nearly two hours. The bus for the next leg of the journey to Mannarkkad was filling up gradually, and the conductor was in no hurry to leave so long as even a few of the seats remained unoccupied, hailing potential passengers to his vehicle in a loud and mechanical voice threatening imminent departure:

'Mannarkka—Mannarkka—Mannnarkkad....'

By the time the driver finally started the engine and the bus began to move—out of the crowded city depot and through narrow streets before turning off on the highway—every seat was taken and there were a few standing passengers too.

Despite all the bumps and violent lurches at sharp curves and hairpin bends, once they had begun to climb Nirmala did manage to doze off, though her mind kept wandering. In the end she slept soundly for nearly three hours until woken up by the sudden hubbub of passengers alighting and vendors fiercely proclaiming their wares inside the paved and roofed plaza of a stylish, brand-new bus depot. In a daze, she realized they had reached Mannarkkad. She stirred drowsily in her seat, but it took a few moments to shrug off inertia before she could reach up and collect her small overnight bag from the luggage rack.

In barely a few minutes, she was travelling to the Attappady forest in an open jeep packed mostly with tribals. But, Nirmala noticed, there were no Kurumbas among them. From the design of the heavy nose rings on two women sitting across her, she guessed these were probably Irulas, and from the style of the sari knotted behind her neck that one must be a Mudugar. Her knowledge of tribal habits and customs was pretty inadequate, she realized, for her to be sure. Under her curious gaze, the other women smiled at her, recognizing her as one of their own.

The driver of the packed taxi-jeep had informed Nirmala when she boarded that Edavani would come almost at the end of the journey. Although each of them did have a tiny portion of wooden bench to squeeze into, the passengers were pretty cramped.

They had covered a fairly large distance—maybe an hour-and-a-half's drive, when the jeep stopped for about ten minutes at a small roadside tea-and-coffee stall. Everyone alighted, glad for a chance to stretch and quaff a hot coffee. It was already evening.

Before partaking of refreshment or inhaling the fresh mountain air deeply, almost all the tribal people devoted a moment to prayer, quietly bowing their heads, to a mountain peak looming over them a short distance away: shaped like a giant Shivalingam, this was Malleswaram Mudi. The name came back to Nirmala in a flash—her mother had pointed it out when she was so very little—it was perhaps her earliest memory.

Much goodness emanated from this natural formation of an enormous Shiva temple, Kishori had told her. The blessings that the Kurumba, Irulas, Mudugars and other tribal people believed accrued to those who worshipped at this shrine could be life-transforming indeed. After silent enunciation of their deepest desires, each of the tribal people touched a hand gratefully to the heart, and laughed aloud with palpable relief that they had covered more than half their journey and almost reached their

The Prospect of Miracles

destination safely.

Nirmala bought two sweet biscuits of yellowish hue, dipping them in her coffee and munching slowly. Presently the driver of the jeep who had been missing all this while returned to the vehicle, urging passengers rather impatiently to get back in so they could resume their journey. Once they had reluctantly complied, he did a head count and discovered they were short by one. Before he could begin to yell out for the missing party, a woman and her small child stepped up from behind a distant clump of bushes.

'Come on, come on!' yelled the driver rudely. 'It will soon be night, and I'll have to stay over in Bhootyoor or Kadaambi. I don't like to drive back in pitch-dark.'

'There'll be a good half-moon, sir, don't you worry,' a chatty old woman contradicted him. 'The night of Shiva's still eight days away. And besides, it will only be in the morning you'll be able to round-up half dozen passengers to carry back to Mannarkkad. So drive slowly, please.'

To that the driver didn't reply, merely resumed his driving with grim attentiveness and greater caution, following the narrow, shadowy, and sometimes meandering but always ascending road through thick deciduous woods and lush dark bush. The great silence of the forest rendered the darkness deeper, and everyone remained silent. Occasionally the passengers in the jeep caught a glimpse of the rays of a declining sun, glimmering through thick foliage, or heard the shriek of a solitary bird settling down for the night.

When Nirmala reached Edavani, dusk had already turned to deep indigo, two hours ago. Nevertheless, in the village a small bonfire was blazing, around which sat a group of people. A couple of them stood up when they saw a strange girl approaching.

Nirmala was well-received and directed to her Uncle Sonu and Aunt Sitladevi's hut once she told them who she was, where she had come from.

Despite the gloom that pervaded the thatched dwelling of her ailing aunt's family, with the medicine-man and diviner having both conceded that her time had come—that she might not have more than a few days, possibly but a few hours left to live—her relatives took pains not to let Nirmala feel infected by the family's sorrow, and first offered her something to eat. But Nirmala wasn't hungry, just very tired after the long journey.

She was soon introduced to another young girl, Chandrika, her first cousin. Although she was feeling too exhausted for a lengthy conversation, it was like meeting a long lost friend, and they embraced spontaneously several times.

Nirmala had brought along a rolled-up cane mat to lie on and a sheet to cover herself. She retrieved them from her bag.

Her uncle showed her where she could make her bed inside their hut, but Nirmala thought it a better idea to sleep in the open fenced-in area just outside. Within minutes of stretching out on the mat, she was fast asleep.

(vii)

A chorus of birdsong and awakening forest life roused her pleasantly at dawn.

Still tired, but rested now, Nirmala found herself being peered at from a distance by a very old woman.

Inhabitants of the village were already up and about. She hadn't been introduced to members of Sitladevi's family the previous night, but guessed this old crone who was coughing away might be her Uncle Sonu's mother, well over eighty years old, and a habitual ganja-smoker of whom she had heard mention even in faraway Kanjirappally.

Legendary for her ability to enter into prolonged trances, cast spells, make predictions, always called on to adjudicate in the event of a theft, she was famous for being able to unearth the truth or divine the whereabouts of missing goods.

Nirmala stood and rolled up her mat.

She smiled at the old woman, who continued to gaze at her with a peculiarly piercing squint. She didn't smile back, although it would have been difficult to tell if she had, given that her face was a mass of intense wrinkles. The bent old woman shuffled up to Nirmala and, with a mighty effort, stood herself upright and held Nirmala's face tenderly in her hands.

'What is it, child? You were crying so much at night? I heard you in your sleep, sighing and whimpering so bitterly…. Why, do you remember?'

'I think I was just very tired, Amma,' said Nirmala sorrowfully, but even as she made that excuse she felt overcome, as though she might burst into tears.

'Have some hot tea. It will give you strength. Then you can tell me the truth—if you want to,' said the old woman, caressing her face once more with great kindness.

The days passed swiftly amidst preparations of dried meat and fermented drink for the great feast—to which Nirmala, like everyone else in the village contributed hours of practical assistance—and soon it was the night of Shiva, an unending celebration of eating and drinking and laughter and dance that extended through the night and well after the golden rays of dawn had drenched the merriment of the village folk in recurring waves of stimulation and exhaustion.

For Nirmala it was an incredible twelve hours in which she laughed a lot and wept and danced and drank copious amounts of toddy as well as stronger liquor. By the morning she had made good friends with Chandrika, whom she began to think of as the younger sister she never had.

Chandrika herself was completely exuberant and overjoyed because, as everyone in the family and village observed, Shiva's glorious benedictions had wrought such vast improvement in Sitladevi's condition somehow, that on the next and subsequent mornings, contrary to a host of bleak prognoses, it was clear she wasn't going to die as yet. In fact, she was steadily regaining her strength.

Nirmala had stayed away from Daeva Danam for nearly two months. Of course, Edavani was her real home in a sense, and she had relished every moment she spent there.

Apart from Chandrika, she also grew very close to Uncle Sonu's aged mother, and spent hours talking to her in a most candid manner, about her life at the farm which was located almost forty kilometres from Kanjirappally, as well as about the old woman's own life in the forest. She was preparing to make the long journey back in a day or two, when Sonu and his wife and their other relations asked Nirmala if she would take Chandrika back with her to the plantation. She was wasting away here in Attappady, they said, instead of becoming smarter like Nirmala herself had in closer proximity to a big town. Nirmala readily agreed.

It was an idea she had herself planted during her rambles in the forest with Chandrika.

III

MOONLIGHTING

11

By the time the girls returned to Daeva Danam from Attappady, Pius was rather well-settled in his workroom, using it several hours every day in the late evening or night.

Making notes, he had explained to me, for a book of religious discourse—but in succinct format: mainly epigrams and homilies. Unfortunately for him, it was to remain a work in progress, or it might have made a nice companion volume to his *Everyday Sermons*. But for this he had only himself to blame, that he frittered away so much time in brutish sensualism.

Nirmala had been away for so long that I was at the end of my tether trying to cope with housework, cooking and whatnot when I received a phone call from her. In response to a long-standing grouse she would surely have heard me ventilate quite often—about inadequate help for me on the farm—she asked me if she could bring along her cousin from Edavani, Chandrika.

'Where are you speaking from?' was the first question I put to her.

'An STD booth in Mannarkkad,' she replied. 'Uncle Sonu had some work here, and he brought us along just to make this phone call.'

'And how long do you think before you get back to Kanjirappally?'

'Soon, Amma, very soon. Is a week okay?'

Barely fourteen when she arrived, Chandrika took a while to adjust to our more urbanized ways. In only a couple of weeks, however, she showed her mettle, and became almost as efficient and capable as Nirmala herself.

A lovely child, unusually pale-skinned and quick to smile, her sunny disposition glowing as it must have on the full-moon night when she was born in the forest: for which reason her mother had decided to name her Chandrika.

Much later, I was to discover that Pius, only a few years after Mark came into this world, had made it a fairly regular habit to summon Nirmala to his workroom at night while the rest of us on the farm were fast asleep; as Chacko had summoned her mother to his bedroom in earlier days—although perhaps, Kishori and he, faced only with Rosalie's helpless submission, may have been practically living together.

When this liaison began Nirmala would have been no more than seventeen. It was clear to me that given the sexual ecstasies Pius would have lavished on the ingénue tribal girl, beginning with her very first experience at his hands on that electric moonlit night when they waited for hours in the dark for a tube he had fitted to flicker to life, Nirmala was likely to have become entirely besotted by the Pastor's enchanting capacity to bestow unimaginable pleasures on her.

As was his wont, Pius did not use this relationship merely to satisfy his sexual gluttony, but also—in the process mitigating some of the guilt arising out of it—to introduce her to Christian beliefs and encouraging her to be baptized in the name of Jesus Christ!

In the initial stages of this informal compact, I can hardly blame Nirmala if, in the privacy of her fantasies, she saw herself as the Pastor's undeclared, unsung wife, who might perhaps one day replace her predecessor.

Yet, illusions of love provided little solace; not imbued as they were with affinity or affection, their intimacies could never have sustained years of mechanical sexual servitude to a man in late middle age. She was too sensible not to realize Pius was simply using her.

But the moment of reckoning when the mired root of habitual indulgence would be fiercely wrenched out came sooner than the Pastor could imagine or anticipate.

Nor should I have been terribly surprised if, five years down the line, Chandrika, now a nubile and gorgeous nineteen, attracted Pius's overwhelming interest—albeit Pius, during those days was much harassed by chronic lumbago. Nirmala, I recall, approached me one evening and held out a fairly large plastic packet containing a fine grey powder. It was a tribal Kurumba formulation, she proudly admitted, but very effective, and would definitely alleviate the Pastor's lumbar pains.

Since that first visit at the end of which she had brought her cousin back with her, Nirmala and Chandrika had travelled once more to Attappady in the intervening years after Chandrika's mother passed away.

It was on their return journey from Edavani, the second time, that Nirmala brought back this smooth grey herbal concoction. It had been specially prepared for her by the old woman, her uncle's mother, she told me, while also making a cautionary suggestion:

'Only thing you should keep in mind,' she said, handing over the plastic packet, 'is that this medicine works very slowly. It may take four months before it starts showing results…but then, for a lifetime you will be rid of this problem….'

And the Pastor, she elaborated, given his modern, impetuous

ways, would surely lose patience before allowing the medicine its requisite span of time to work. It might be better, she suggested, to not draw his attention to it at all. Distilled and later calcified from rare herbs found in the forest of Attappady, the medicine was in any case tasteless: just a half teaspoon mixed in his dinner every night would surely give commendable results over time.

It was a dark, overcast evening, I remember. In the distance I could see the white glow of the tube-light she had left on in her hut, which she now shared with Chandrika.

Just then, a roll of thunder and smattering of rain, suddenly it was dark as night and severely overcast. I stood watching Nirmala's slim brown body as she traced her way back to her shack, hips swaying with youthful abandon. Over the last fifty yards or so, she had to sprint: the rain was coming down in torrential gusts now.

Could I already have been so dull in the head as to not suspect something fishy? Even when she had enjoined secrecy on my feeding the powder to Pastor? It was weeks before the deterioration in his condition became apparent to me.

By then, the routine for preparing his dinner tray had become invariable—I got it ready for him myself, had done so even in the past; he liked to take his dinner much earlier than I did and, for him, a small portion of rice at night was a must.

He never suspected a thing.

12

At the heart of our universe broods meaning.

Not quite so cryptic or indecipherable as one might imagine: deep and genuine questing is the sole leaven demanded of those who seek to know.

Now the Pastor's not around, I am free again.

Already, I sense great power surging through my veins: I feel more capable, more in control of my quest. And no longer do I have to contend with his insinuations, his constant jibes about my personal habits that reflected, according to him, my lack of mental rigour, my self-indulgence, my excitability....

∽

Yes, it's true he's gone—for good, I suppose—but before he went, he made sure to leave behind a lackey to keep close watch over me.

And this hireling of his, Thomachen, claims to be in diurnal spiritual rapport with the Pastor!

I find his presence on the plantation intolerable.

Not that he deliberately tries to irritate me. In fact, probably aware of my dislike for him—and with Pastor gone his tenure that much more uncertain—he keeps out of my way.

But precisely because he doesn't want attention drawn to

himself, he behaves in the most appalling ways. Tiptoes around the place, speaks only in whispers if he speaks at all, strives to pale into invisibility yet, through excessive self-deprecation only succeeds in making himself all the more ridiculous: a proper nuisance.

None of this explains why I should have behaved so vengefully, so spitefully with him. But that came a little later.

∽

All that cruelty and hatred, the massive sense of mortification I had embraced when, against better counsel, I decided to marry Pius…thank God it's all over….

Mark, where are you? It's you I miss. When you went away, I would never have imagined this was to be a permanent separation.

Only when one is down in the dumps, when everything's lost, humility wrestles free: embodying in essence perhaps the soul's deepest and most fragile substance.

∽

A blessing indeed that life sputtered out of Pastor when it did—just as it did; or he would have been greatly encumbered by the weight of surviving these ghastly times.

If you remember—oh yes, I do—it was Pius himself who first introduced the idea to you: the enigma of end times, as he called it, how imminent it could be.

But then as he gained favour and praise with parishioners and his superiors in the ministry, he was lulled into complacence and a gloating pride, his own need to understand God's design blunted, instead of becoming keener.

And more than anything else, his predilection for illicit pleasure—the enormity of his addiction to it—that was to be his final undoing.

Had he a chance to trudge a trifle further down the sorry course of his self-indulgent life, he might have gained better hold on his senses, read the signs accurately, atoned for his sins.

But that wasn't to be—he wasn't given time for reparation.

I remember an earlier phase in our life together when he'd pore over the Word of God diligently every evening after dinner: a few verses of scripture, sometimes a psalm or a proverb. He would read it to himself or aloud to Mark and me, then reflect on it with a few well-chosen words: and I would admire how well he knew his Bible.

But towards the end even that had stopped: he withdrew so much into himself and that wretched workroom of his, he had given up everything.... Or some of those verses would surely have jogged his memory, inspired him to judge his hollow successes more severely. I suspect, too, that in the confines of that gloomy shack, in his last days he had developed a secret taste for alcohol.

Does that amaze you? His physical discomfort too may have been growing by then. Outwardly though, there were hardly any signs of distress: fine wrinkles that had begun to appear on his smooth skin, and very poor digestion.

∽

This know also, that in the last days perilous times shall come.... For men shall become lovers of their own selves, covetous, boasters, proud, blasphemers, disobedient to parents, unthankful...incontinent, fierce, despisers of those that are good...lovers of pleasures more than lovers of God....

If I'm not mistaken—oh you know very well you're not, stop being disingenuous!—no doubt then, as you say, I do know: 2 Timothy. Chapter 3, Verse 2....

I learned much from Pius, I won't lie.

The Prospect of Miracles

I remember in one of his first sermons which I would have heard more than twenty years ago, he spoke of the human longing for God, for transcending 'loneliness of self', for re-immersion in Godhead.

Then again, in another, he had quoted an Islamic mystic of the Middle Ages. I was most impressed by his eclectic and vast resources. 'I sought God for thirty years,' the Sufi saint is reported to have said. 'I thought it was I who desired Him. But no, it was He who desired me.'

And more recently, one Sunday morning Pastor delivered an angry sermon on sexual mores in our society: why populist depictions—movies, books, cultural preferences, which justify and even promote sexual promiscuity as being psychologically healthy—were indeed bizarre: that they could not but be completely abhorrent to God.

'Every couple, every man, every woman, in God's scheme of things is unique and irreplaceable.... Their equivalence is something that's divinely ordained, a perfect unity joined by holy matrimony—not something that's interchangeable, like a game of musical chairs!' he had thundered from the podium of the rented hall where the service was taking place.

'...When man and woman come together in love, they become, as the Bible describes it: one flesh, every external facet of their lives, every interiority, too, is united in the mystery of love.

'If, outside of marriage you are sexually attracted to another individual, that's all very well, but ask yourself first before you act—will I be able to embrace and cherish every single bone and muscle of this body? Every single wistful longing in his or her heart?

'For that is the order of God's expectation from us, nothing short of that. You cannot say: Lord, my desire for this man or woman is driving me crazy. It may be temporary, but I can't help myself...let me just make love to her. Just this once, may I?'

It boggles the mind that the Pastor, my late husband, could have lacked self-reflection so completely as to be able to hold forth in this pietistic vein—or else had adjusted himself to being so profoundly, so solemnly hypocritical!

∽

In his absence, I do feel less constrained, better able, in a manner of speaking, to take his place...!

Not officially, of course; by no means. A new pastor is on his way, so I've heard. For some reason, his arrival in Kottayam has been delayed.

But willy-nilly, a small coterie of acquaintances and friends has begun to gather around me—like moths to a flame?—hoping perhaps that some of my late husband's moral rectitude has rubbed off. Not even a handful of his admirers suspect how hollow and hypocritical all those purported claims to sainthood on Pius's behalf are—inspired elocutionary prowess, yes, none would deny him that—on occasion he could speak brilliantly—but in essence he was a totally selfish man, vain enough to believe he had a special connection with God: such a coward and hypocrite.

What was it he hoped to discover about the world or himself by having sex with a girl young enough to be his daughter?

An elixir for waning, rickety youth?

Essentially he could have been a better man, had he not loved himself so much—more than he could his wife, or for that matter, his God.

Yes, there's anger and bitterness, perhaps even hatred, if it's possible for these to continue simmering retrospectively. But at

The Prospect of Miracles

least the terrible unhappiness of enforced togetherness is over, and I'm alone once again.

∽

In truth, the time has come for me to declare something quite astounding: the Lord has been good to me, He has entrusted me with something so wonderfully unique—ah, much more than anything Pius could possibly have had to offer the world—which will make it sit up and take notice in sheer stupefaction!

This latter-day miracle I have kept under wraps for a few days now—but only yesterday the Lord instructed me in no unclear terms that the time was ripe for all to hear and comprehend. I can hardly stop marvelling at just how blessed I am to be chosen as conduit for His transmissions.

I, Mary Agnes, among all the millions of women and millions of Marys in the world, have been appointed receptacle of His Grace, amanuensis for the final olive branch He is offering humanity before the seventh trumpet is sounded—our last chance that is, before the triumphant final act is played out amid cataclysmic displays of His power and glory: when every last gasp of life on Earth is extinguished!

The signs are everywhere, you'll agree: one need only glance at the morning papers and the headlines sock you right in the eye: wars, famines, unprecedented floods, earthquakes, unquenchable forest fires, you name it: and towering above all manner of natural disaster, those terrorist groups that straddle the face of the globe, each demanding their obdurate pound—kilos—of flesh!

Poor Parveen. Islamic State and the war in Syria collided with her in a most horrible way, swallowing her two young boys in its infernal pathway.

In our own country too, even here in Kerala, signs of ugliness, intolerance and devilish frenzy are growing rapidly.

Just two days ago a Christian cemetery was desecrated, and yet another church set on fire (the flames doused by a sacristan, fortunately, before much damage could be done). And then there was that other case last year, of a college lecturer whose hands were chopped off at the wrist—punishment exacted by foot soldiers of a fundamentalist outfit owing allegiance to his own creed, Islam, for publicly expounding liberal views to his students in class.

It's commonsensical, isn't it? No accident all this carnage is being heaped on mankind right now more frequently; an unrelenting tsunami of cosmic misfortune: these are the wages of sin, long accrued on humanity's ledger, never honoured, never defrayed. What befell Sodom and Gomorrah was laughably insignificant in comparison: and that was so very long ago, one can only marvel at the extent of His patience with mankind.

But for sure it's running out. Our time, His patience.

IV

MARY HEARS THE VOICE OF GOD

13

For the sake of posterity—is there any such postulate still left to speak of?—I want to document just how I began to receive messages from God, and what their content has been, what it is He wants us so desperately to grasp. If I describe the very first time He spoke to me, you may prefer to believe—some of you—that I am prey to fantasy.

Or, if more charitably inclined, explain it in terms of epiphany, or a momentary, but self-induced illumination. Ah, Pius wouldn't have minced his words: nothing short of delusion, he would have declared!

But never before have I laid claim to gifts of prophecy or divination or anything of that sort. These phrases too, seem completely inaccurate descriptions of my particular experience: the unavoidable and simple truth, I am compelled to conclude, is that Jesus chose me to record significant dispatches He wants humanity to receive. And, if possible—this means I suppose He does retain some shred of hope—that humanity may heed His warning: for no known merit I can lay claim to, I have been endowed with the exalted status of being his final prophet.

Now I must clarify again: the very first time it happened I could hardly believe it myself, that it was He! Could I have imagined the whole thing then? And should I blame myself for my initial incredulity?

Not at all; because on that first occasion, the transmission came upon me while I was still in my sleep. Even so, such a profound and amazing experience!

ᔕ

At one moment it was night, and I was deep in slumber; in the next I was carried aloft on a wave of paranormal or perhaps divine energy.

I knew at once it wasn't a dream. I felt instantly wide awake! And if anyone should contend that such extravagant creative fancies are the very stuff of our subconscious, I can only say in my defence—if a dream, then it was one played out on such a sublimely expansive scale, on so grandly magnificent a 'dream set' such as never designed or imagined before! Besides being shot through with 'special effects' such as Hollywood's most legendary cinematic wizards could never have mobilized—no, far beyond anything that human agency could conceive or contrive—let alone my own pitiful subconscious; nor anything I will ever be able to adequately describe in words.

My beloved daughter.... My dear Mary Agnes....

When I heard that deep resonant voice suffused with kindness, I sensed immediately who was speaking. Neither amazed, nor afraid, His Voice engulfed me entirely—I was apprehending it not with my ears alone, but with every part of my being, electrified.

As one who has known suffering and how to abide by it, please understand I have something very important to ask of you.... You can be of immense help to me in this difficult hour.... My trials on the Cross can't compare with the sorrows I now must bear every moment, knowing how smugly Satan sits and watches humanity drift toward certain doom. Know this, dear daughter: My Father in Heaven is terribly angry with the world, with how man has ignored, distorted and perverted His most fundamental commandments; and moreover, defiled the very Earth that He so meticulously imagined and created; He had envisaged it, even after the Fall, as a second Paradise for man to inhabit.

I do not have the power, or for that matter, conviction—to be honest with you—to prevail on Him, to beseech greater patience of Him. But if you are ready to help, perhaps we can save a handful of souls....

On that first occasion His message remained fairly concise and brief. When the Voice faded away, I didn't feel like I was waking up from a dream—on the contrary, I felt great agitation as though emerging from some convulsion or seizure—more precisely, I suppose, from a super-essential spiritual cleansing that had transformed me forever. It took me a few minutes to feel normal again.

Naturally, after that I didn't go back to sleep. I got out of bed—it must have been almost morning, I remember hearing the very faint chirping of birds—and turned on the light. Then, I began to jot down the Words of our Lord, as precisely I could, as He had instructed me to:

You can help me by recording all that I say to you, and sharing it with the world. So that all may have a chance to know how close the End is. Unless you repent now, you will be lost forever to the Evil One who waits patiently to reap a rich harvest of souls, please tell them.... Many will not believe you, many will ridicule your claims and call you a dreamer. But be ready to make that sacrifice for me, be prepared for calumny....

Yes, I think I have reproduced His Words accurately. And I

am prepared for the worst forms of mockery and derision.

∽

I won't boast rock-solid conviction from the start. I have to confess perplexity and self-doubt.

But just one more communication from the Lord was all it took for me to feel reassured that Jesus was indeed speaking to me.

And this time, as though to dispel every vestige of irresolute belief, He spoke to me by the harsh light of day. No aerial transportation through masses of cloud, no histrionic sound and light displays; nor did He pick on any fanciful or mysterious setting for this transmission—such as the misty hills of Munnar, or the oceanic expanses of Lake Vembanad just a few miles away. Perhaps that was what finally convinced me.

My burning bush, as it were, had ignited in the midst of hardcore reality, that is, my own humdrum existence at the plantation of Daeva Danam, no more than a half-hour's drive from Periyar Tiger Reserve.

But even on that second occasion—and this seems to happen every single time He addresses me now—instantly, I felt I was entering a trance:

My dearest daughter, Mary Agnes...I am sorry to burden you with such grave responsibilities. But frightening times will soon be upon us.... Nation shall rise against nation, and kingdom against kingdom: and there shall be wars and famines, pestilences, and earthquakes in diverse places.

In these latter times, many shall depart from the faith, giving heed to seducing spirits, and doctrines of devils. And there shall be signs in the sun, and in the moon, and in the stars; and upon the earth great distress of nations.... No, I cannot say exactly when....

Of that day and hour knoweth no man, no, not the angels of heaven, but My Father only.

Watch therefore, be ye also ready: when these things start to happen, stand up and lift your heads because your redemption is drawing near....

Thank you, O Lord, for your timely warnings, I whispered to myself when His Voice faded away.

Thank you also for computers, and the internet, which will enable me to disseminate Your messages swiftly and widely, so all can read and gain time to reflect on Your admonitions—as you have Yourself suggested, if I remember right, I will conceal my identity and remain anonymous; the messenger does not signify so much as the message.

I have decided to call my website TheLastProphet.com. Is that an auspicious term, do you think, Lord? Please bless this journey I undertake in Thy Holy Name....

V
BACKWATERS

14

At around four-thirty that afternoon, which was the time he had given me, I heard the faint bump of a car entering the farm, meandering through twists and turns in the driveway before coming to a halt outside the living room cottage.

I waited until I heard the car door open and slam shut—once, twice?—only then stepped out to greet my visitor. It was the new pastor: he had telephoned that morning to ask if he could drop by and pay his condolences.

But I saw now that he hadn't come alone.

☙

Older than any of us had expected—hair thinning and grey at the temples—he stood like a statue, stationary at the threshold of the living room, hands joined in a respectful pranam.

'Forgive us, madam, hope we are not intruding too much. I am Kae Perambil. And this, my young friend Sudarshan, whom I took the liberty of bringing along.'

The young man accompanying Perambil was probably thirty or just under: a stunning good-looker at that, tall, with long curly locks of hair. He had hung back initially, but as soon as he was introduced stepped up, and joined his hands in imitation of the pastor.

'Perambil? Never heard that name before. Whereabouts are you from?'

'Well, it's a long story,' said the pastor. 'My great-grandfather hailed from a village near Sriperumbudur, south of Chennai. Only in the last generation his grandson, that is, my father decided to migrate from Tamil Nadu to north Kerala.'

'So then what's the K for? I thought that would stand for your village or native place?'

'Oh no, no! Kae is my first name. K-a-e,' he spelt it out. 'I always have to explain this when I meet someone the first time. You see, Kae, as you know, means the Lord in Malayalam. My mother was convinced she would never have any children. Until, after much penance and prayer, she did conceive. By then Father was already finalizing plans for shifting to Kerala. In gratitude for His Mercy, my parents decided to christen me with a Malayali first name!

'And Sudarshan, of course, you must have seen before. He's actually a resident of Kottayam city, though he travels a lot; a great admirer of your late husband....'

I had never set eyes on the young man before, although the shock of curls on his head reminded me of Pius in his younger days. But Sudarshan claimed to have heard Pius preach on two occasions at the old church, in the days before it was attacked by hooligans.

'A great man...a very great man, if I may say so....'

He was full of praise for Pius.

'I was so moved when I heard him preach, I believe it really changed me, or at least, re-orientated my life.... When Pastor Perambil told me he was on his way to meet you, I begged of him to let me come along. You see, I never had a chance to actually get to know the late Pastor personally. Or to thank him for what he did for me—without even being aware of my existence, actually! So I thought, while I have this chance I should meet his wife at least....'

Suave. Clearly a charmer.

'Now his widow, sadly,' I corrected him, and smiled, 'but you are most welcome.'

Parvati had kept the tea service ready. As I poured out three cups of steaming tea from the ceramic pot, I was seized with a strong intuition: so attractive and personable yet, I thought to myself, I have to stay wary of this Sudarshan; can't trust him at all....

Perhaps I should have lent greater credence to my preliminary hunch, but instead, as we indulged in small talk—about Pius, and his now widespread reputation as a wise and compassionate pastor, as also problems of Christians in our parish, and indeed the whole country, I allowed good looks and immaculate demeanour to work their spell on me.

Only much later did I discover a basic deception to his story—he had begun by introducing himself as a computer engineer—only partially untrue, I suppose, he does know a lot about computers, internet and so on, but what he failed to mention was that he was essentially a freelance journalist who had, by chance, come across my website on the Net. And its three current posts aroused his curiosity considerably, so that he was in the process of employing every device, technical and detectional to uncover who 'The Last Prophet' could possibly be! He thought it would make for a fantastic news story.

Something about his manner had got my sixth sense tingling, I should have paid more attention to it but didn't.

That first meeting, predominated by exchanges of pleasantries between the three of us, was so reassuring that before I knew it the presentiment receded and had faded away.

In any case, on that first day my visitors were with me for a very brief while.

When they had sipped their tea, and eaten a slice each of plum cake—from our local bakery down in Kanjirappally.... M'mm, not bad at all, said Pastor Perambil.... In fact, insisted Sudarshan, extremely nice.... Both men, presently assumed a tragically glum air as they made ponderous enquiries into Pius's terminal illness.

'Oh, it was one of those lingering malaises I'm afraid, which lasted months,' I told them. 'Doctors tried everything, of course, but never quite managed a definitive diagnosis.... Every few days Pius would himself say to me, "Agnes, I am feeling so much better now, I am getting well."

'But in point of fact, he never really improved. Those last two months it was all steadily downhill, and then suddenly one night—he was gone. Anyway, now you're here at least our parishioners won't be deprived of a pastor, as they have been all these months. Though myself, I suppose I will continue to miss Pius for a very long time....'

In that moment, I too was able to pretend to wipe away incipient tears....

'Can I pour you one more cup?'

'Of course you will, my dear, of course...and no doubt some of the parishioners too.... Tea? Do we have time, Sudarshan?'

'Not for me, thanks. I'm good,' said Sudarshan.

'You see, we have to make a few more home visits after this one,' said the pastor. 'But I'm so glad, so very glad for this chance to make your acquaintance, madam.'

'Please don't call me that! I'm Mary. Mary Agnes.'

'Likewise, Mary Agnes,' said Sudarshan. 'Wonderful to have

met you....'

In a few minutes they took their leave, thanked me again for seeing them and left. I couldn't understand why I was feeling so hot and bothered, and at the same time relieved they had gone.

How odd that so superficial a reference to Pius's morbidity in discussion with two strangers should have had such a disconcerting effect on me?

Or was it Sudarshan?

Was it meeting him that agitated me so? Do keep a hold on yourself, Mary Agnes. He's at least fifteen years your junior! But isn't that precisely why? Oh, this is amazing.... What's happening to you? Have you been so terribly deprived of male companionship since Pius left? And it's been hardly a few months since the curtain fell so hard on him, Mary.

Perhaps this was exactly how Pius felt when he was enamoured of that young slip, Nirmala? Exactly what frivolous fancies are you indulging in now, Mary Agnes? Do get a hold on yourself!

Anyway, haven't you noticed? Nobody compliments you anymore for the beauty you once supposedly possessed. Glanced at yourself in the mirror, lately? Old hag!

∽

I would have too, I'm sure, got a hold on myself, banished such frivolous fancies —had I been given a day or two to compose myself.

But believe it or not, the very next morning, Sudarshan phoned and asked me if we could meet again.

What about, I asked, and didn't need to feign surprise.

Well, there's something important I need to discuss with you. It wouldn't have been proper for me to bring it up yesterday, since we had only just met. But this time around, if you're willing, we could meet outside somewhere, have a nice meal perhaps at some quiet restaurant—of your choice, of course—where we could talk at length, without distraction or interruption.

Of course, put like that my curiosity was terribly provoked, but I decided not to give in so easily.

I thought we had talked all we could only yesterday, until there was nothing more left to say. But even as I conveyed that to him, I had decided on Marina: a fish place that had opened recently in Kanjirappally and become quite the talk of town. I had been thinking I should try it out.

I pretended it would be impossible for me to meet him in the next ten days, at least. Well, I really was very busy, and didn't want to seem too willing. I had a new post to write for my website—I did this almost every week now—because God had not remained silent, His urgency compels me to keep pace.

And I must say, recent events in my life had filled me with a stronger sense of self-worth than any experience I could recall in my remotest past.

∽

Last night Jesus spoke to me, this time too in my sleep.

But His Words were branded in my psyche with shockingly unquestionable precision—as soon as I bounced out of bed I wrote the message down, word for word:

My dearest daughter, how brilliant so many of you on Earth are, how well you conduct yourselves.

But of the heart's simplicity—basic humility—even tiny fragments are hard to come by. And this very smartness, this glorification of human intelligence, has steered humanity to pride, swank and swollen headedness! The very sin that led to the fall of the angels....

How well you fathom all of Creation, indeed manipulate it.

But you forget the Beast chuckling away in the wings, waiting to have the last laugh.

If you had saved a little room in your hearts to feel my Divine Grace, so much suffering and sorrow could have been averted.

This is only the beginning, be assured. Alas, much worse is yet to come....

Pius? Are you out there? Are you aware of all that's happening to me? I wonder what you think of me now.

15

Before agreeing to see Sudarshan for lunch, I spent hours brooding on the propriety of consenting to such a request. In the end I had to admit I was simply dying to, not least out of curiosity to find out what it was he wanted to speak to me about.

Some telephonic persistence from Sudarshan may have helped clinch the issue, but finally I decided I didn't care two hoots what people might say about our date. And since he himself had insisted we meet at a restaurant of my choice, Marina it would be after all.

On later reflection though—days and weeks after the relationship had gone up in smoke—I realized perhaps I had been hasty, too trusting of this young man.

∽

That afternoon when I stepped out of a taxi in front of the Marina's façade, I realized I was arriving a full twenty-five minutes late. But then the distance is considerable: Daeva Danam to Kanjirappally is almost an hour's drive.

The steward who escorted me in seemed to know which table I was expected at.

In any case very few were occupied—only one other couple,

and a large, somewhat boisterous family of six. In a secluded nook of the spacious but deserted rotisserie sat Sudarshan: a bottle of chilled rosé before him.

He got up to greet me as soon as he saw me approach, shook hands rather vigorously while expansively brushing aside my apologies for being late.

'It's me who should apologize, really—not to have had the patience to wait and first ask what you'd like to drink—I was feeling just so parched…. And once the bottle was brought to my table…ah, so tempting to open and start sipping it. It's very nice wine. But perhaps you would prefer something else?'

'I'm afraid I never drink.'

This came across perhaps with more severity than intended, so that the young man who had been savouring his rosé became instantly abashed and apologetic. But perhaps I was only echoing the Pastor's own obdurate principles.

'To tell you the truth, I don't often drink myself. And almost never during the day. But today, like I said, I was feeling so thirsty…and so—well, *perturbed* really…perhaps a little unsure of myself too: about all the things I want to discuss with you. I should never have started before you arrived—please forgive me.'

'Oh no, it's okay, believe me. You don't need to apologize,' I said. 'I'm sorry I kept you waiting so long. But I'm curious: what was it you couldn't have discussed with me when you came over with Pastor Perambil?'

Had it been just a pretext for meeting again, all those phone calls about an urgent matter that couldn't wait? I suspected something of the sort; for Sudarshan seemed in no hurry to raise any contentious topic of discussion, nor did he provide any substance to justify his compellingly alarmist calls.

The Prospect of Miracles

'It's very nice in here, isn't it?' he said. 'Ah, so cool and relaxing....'

Not until he had poured himself some more wine and consumed a deep draught.

'Well, I've been wondering you see...and somehow I thought, as the late pastor's wife, you would be the best person to discuss all this with.'

'All what?'

'I'm coming to that...give me only a minute or two.... Do you think, Mary Agnes,' here he sipped his glass again and took another long pause, 'it makes sense to refer back to a book written 2,000 years ago to explain what's happening to us now?'

'How do you mean?'

'Well, this terrible thirst I'm feeling at all times, for one thing—that's what set me thinking on these lines. Not just today, for months now.... And the heat, don't forget the heat! I'm not the only one who feels it, of course.... And with every passing year it gets worse and worse. Don't you think so, too?

'Well, not in this air-conditioned restaurant certainly. But the heat can be quite terrible in summer, no doubt. And that in itself contributes to the problem, doesn't it?'

'What?'

'The air conditioning!'

'Oh, absolutely...!' said Sudershan. 'Obviously you do know what I'm getting at—there's that ozone hole brooding right above us here in South India. I've begun to wonder, is that what's responsible for this immense sense of thirst, for feeling so enervated at all times...?

'And in that context,' he continued without pausing, 'I can't help but remember a Biblical prediction about the sun being given power to scorch people with fire. Is it going to be like that? Are we all going to soon be cooked alive by the sun's ultraviolet rays?'

'Ah, The Book of Revelation! I'm impressed. You do know Scripture well.'

'Not really. Just a few things here and there have stuck in memory. From the six years I spent in a seminary…'

'Oh, I didn't know you had. How fascinating.'

'Well, you see, we were eight children in the family! When my father died without making provision for her, Mother decided that as eldest I should go into a seminary. At least partly so there was one less hungry mouth to feed!'

'How old were you then?' I asked.

'Just nine,' he replied. 'It wasn't unpleasant or cruel, or anything, by no means. Just very regimented—five o'clock mass every morning, overdoses of Scripture class and hours of reciting litanies mindlessly.

'And then?'

'Luckily, by the time I was fifteen, my uncle, my dad's elder brother, who was in Abu Dhabi returned to Kerala. He had spent twenty years there: and now he was back, a very rich man.… Not fully aware of Mum's plight till then—or preferring to pretend he wasn't, he saw her condition at last in person, and that of my siblings. He decided to adopt us, financially. He was very generous in fact.… So that's when I decided to leave the seminary and opt for secular education.'

'How very interesting.…'

'But coming back to this insufferable heat and thirst—I tell you I feel it 24/7.… As you say, we don't sense it in here right now. But step out and see how hard it hits you! We continue to create greenhouse gases without a thought for our future. And now we have a weirdo in charge of the most powerful nation in the world who claims that climate change is a hoax!'

'Oh, absolutely! We do live in crazy times, there's no doubt about that,' I was beginning to wonder where all this was leading to.

'That ozone hole would have grown humungous by now. Does anyone care? What with all the aerosol cans women use....'

'Oh, don't tell me men don't. When I walked in just now, the whole restaurant smelt fragrant as a fresh chameli garden!'

'I admit it. Honestly, I do. I sweat so much I have to spray myself liberally. Or people would hold their noses and avoid me like the plague. But you have a great one I must say: the nose of a perfumer: to be able to identify what I'm wearing at first sniff....ah. And, apart from everything else, exquisitely shaped, too...so beautiful....'

We gazed at each other in the low-lit, pleasantly air-conditioned restaurant and smiled. I was secretly pleased to find so much congruence between my own concerns and his; I nevertheless squirmed in embarrassment at his brazen flattery.

'Certainly,' I said, 'only a mad man would doubt the planet is in a bad way. Everything contributes. Every form of pollution, vehicular, industrial, aeronautic—thousands of jet planes crisscrossing the skies day and night, missiles being tested in North Korea, wars in Syria and the Ukraine....'

'Conflicts, wars, skirmishes, ah yes...let's not even go there!' said Sudarshan. 'At any given moment there are dozens in progress....'

'Sure. Everything on earth, our entire civilization is headed toward certain catastrophe and self-destruction, without a doubt.... Ah, now I'm beginning to feel thirsty too. '

'What can I get you?'

'What you have here looks lovely. Don't mind trying a wee bit....'

The hovering steward rushed up to fill a fresh glass with the light pink liquid.

'Well, cheers then,' said Sudarshan, clinking his glass against mine, 'to a long and lasting friendship.'

'Cheers,' I smiled. 'To friendship….'

It made me cringe later to think how quickly the afternoon disintegrated into a sham of bombast, game-playing and insincerity. Was that because both of us had come to lunch obtusely nursing narrow issues and concerns we were intent on raising? Or is that the effect alcohol always has on some people?

∽

Oh yes, we were both enjoying the wine and the conversation very much, I'll confess.

It was exciting to find so much consonance in our views. In fact, I was very much in command of this discourse; having given considerable thought to it in recent times it gave me a sense of power to articulate extensively on these issues like a debater or a TV news anchor. Perhaps that's why I was fuelling my exegesis with more wine more than I should have, and at quite a rapid pace too.

'People have forgotten,' I said, 'to honour God's sovereignty over all Creation: over people and nations, over the very course of human history. Great powers and dazzling inventions, all our pathetic human achievements have definitely made us giddy headed. We feel as though we understand everything now, we have become masters of the universe…. But soon a time will come when we will have to face His anger and His might!'

'"Then they will know that I am the Lord,"' quoted Sudarshan, and in almost instantaneous response, I cried out,

'O yea!'

The Prospect of Miracles

In the hushed ambience of Marina, my voice sounded like a high-pitched and exultant hallelujah.

'I was just about to quote those very words myself! This is amazing!'

Unable to contain my excitement, I repeated, '"Then they will know I am the Lord!" You read my mind! Believe me, I was on the verge of saying those very words…sixty-five times! No less than sixty-five times in the Book of Ezekiel He reminds us of this. And here on Earth so many are still unconvinced; that every additional moment we enjoy on the planet is only by the grace and great mercy of our Lord.'

'I do agree, Mary Agnes, I do agree with every word you have said. It's mind-boggling,' said Sudarshan. 'An unrelenting spate of terror attacks…Islamic State…Syria…Afghanistan…Paris, London, Manchester, you name it. And now Iran threatening to nuke Israel out of existence. Even after the alleged nuclear deal with Obama, observers believe it has clandestinely reverted to enriching uranium.

'One can well understand, or imagine at least, what young people in the West must have felt at the height of the Cold War,' he continued excitedly. 'I mean during the Cuban crisis for example. Make love and forget about the morrow—for there may not be any…. Isn't that how the sexual revolution was born in the first place, swamping much of the first world in its tide?'

'Maybe…. A third world war could well start at any moment. But if Russia and Iran were to invade Israel,' I took over where he paused, thinking aloud, projecting into the near future, 'that would be the beginning of the end…. God is going to lead Russia into Israel for the slaughter, it was predicted by Him 2,000 years ago: the formation of the EU, world domination by one power, then Russia's military might destroyed….'

Simultaneously, as words tumbled out of my mouth in a flood of rapt exclamation, a severer line of thought had been spawned, independently as it were of the first track, yet gnawing away rigorously inside my brain:

What's with you, Mary Agnes? Why are you spouting gibberish in this fashion to a young man who's almost a stranger? And to meet him privately like this in a restaurant while guzzling wine? Are you sure no ulterior motive lurks behind your feverish promotion of end times gospel? Was it for this that Jesus chose you to disseminate his message?

But I found myself unstoppable.

'….the confederation of ten European nations will become the ruling world power very soon. And then it will be time for the Abomination of Desolation to begin…and humankind will know for the very first time the true meaning of suffering. Soon after, it will be the hour for the Antichrist to arise. He will be welcomed by all nations as a visionary, a new saviour!'

'Ah, it's all quite amazing and frightening. How well you do know the Bible, I must say, and God's plans for our immediate future!' said Sudarshan. 'By the way, I had been wondering: was Ezekiel the *last prophet* to make an appearance in the Old Testament?'

The sly manner in which he emphasized those two words should have rung an alarm bell in my head. But by then we were both—or at least I can say *I* was—too drunk!

'Oh, no, I think there were others after him…. Hosea, Isaiah, Zechariah….'

'Shall we ask for one last rosé?'

'Don't think I can drink anymore,' I replied, dully. 'Let's order some food, please. Maybe after I get some food in me?'

'Of course, how thoughtless of me,' he apologized. 'This

has been one of the most exciting, thought-provoking lunches I have ever enjoyed. I forgot the time. We've covered so many important topics today, I'm so glad we met.... Oh by the way, I've heard they serve some great grilled lobster here,' said Sudarshan, summoning the waiter who approached us with two oversized menu cards, held open like gargantuan pincers ready to snip at us.

'Why don't you order for both of us, please?' I was suddenly so hungry, I found myself almost pleading for food.

∽

What happened after that I can't remember too well.

I know the seafood was excellent, and we ate a lot of it; once we had finished lunch, Sudarshan helped me into his car and drove me home.

Next thing I knew I had flopped in bed without so much as changing my clothes, although I do remember kicking off my shoes....

It was past six in the evening, and dark outside when I emerged from a deep stupor; I became aware in the same instant of a soft snoring beside me; something heavy was resting on my body.

I shrugged off the hairy arm with surprise and some revulsion, as I sat up still dazed and somewhat shocked.

Sudarshan was fast asleep on my bed.

Fortunately, it was wide enough to afford space for two, without any unseemly huddling.

And I thanked my lucky stars that despite my inebriated condition I hadn't, as I sometimes tend to in steamy weather conditions, stripped off my clothes before crashing out in bed.

16

Peter and Parvati had left early, it appeared.

Nirmala, Chandrika, the old cook, Mariamma, nobody was around. They had all taken the day off in my absence, it would seem. The kitchen was deserted, bare.

And then I saw him: loitering dreamily in the backyard among the rambutan trees.

'Hullo…' I called out to get his attention

'Madam!'

He was taken aback. He'd obviously thought no one but he was around on the property.

'What are you doing here, Thomachen? You're supposed to report for work only in the mornings, am I right? Never after lunch, I had told you. Wasn't that clear to you?'

'Madam—I was just passing by…thought I would check on things—so quiet, nobody around…. I was wondering?'

'Okay, okay—it's okay. Perfect time to snoop around.'

'Madam…?'

Stony incomprehension now vitrified Thomachen's eyes, as always it did in awkward moments.

'It's okay, Thomachen. We'll meet tomorrow.'

I had been sharp with him, and at the back of my mind of course I was also relieved that my own guest was soundly asleep, and unlikely to step out of the bedroom at any moment now....

'Come back in the morning at nine. I have something important to bring to your attention....'

'What? Ammachi—Tell me, please?'

'Morning! Come back in the morning, Thomachen!' I nearly yelled at the man.

Then I walked away from him towards the kitchen, looking back only once to see if he had followed my instructions—oh yes, there he was marching briskly towards the back exit like a subaltern who knows better than to argue with his superiors.

Only after I had made a flask of coffee in the kitchen and taken it back with me to the bedroom did I rouse Sudarshan. He jumped out of bed with a start, looking dazed and sheepish.

The coffee revived us both quickly. We consumed it in guilty silence, like failed conspirators.

'I don't know how to thank you for this wonderful afternoon. Besides everything else, it was also an educative experience for me....'

'Ah...educative?'

'You have great knowledge, great power.... In another time or age,' said Sudarshan, 'you might have been honoured and glorified as a high priestess.'

'Now, you're trying to flatter me....'

'That's not my intention at all,' he shook his head. 'I can't explain myself, I feel so muddled, so exhilarated as well—like a schoolboy who's fallen in love for the first time....'

'Oh, don't be ridiculous,' I laughed. 'Love? It's a long time since anyone used that word with me....'

'I'm not,' he averred rather too emphatically. 'I'm not being silly. I feel totally swept off my feet. Is there anything I can do to prove I mean it?'

And so our banter went on for a while.

I won't try to describe all he did do and say: but the mood I must confess—at least for me, for a while—was one of passivity and wine-induced prurience. That makes me sound like a woman of lax virtue, but the fact is physical intimacy never did come easily to me, and didn't on that day either. But it had been years and years since anyone had actually spoken to me with amorous intent.

I wanted to be touched, to feel loved.

'You do realize how much older I am than you. When you see my flabby, wrinkled body you will feel ashamed—I will, too—and change your mind very quickly....'

In a bizarre way, that's exactly what happened: he had made me feel so admired and beautiful all afternoon, and so much at ease that when he tried to embrace me and kiss my lips, I almost couldn't bring myself to repel him. But then he began to unbutton my shirt and fondle my breasts; and I didn't let him. I firmly pushed him away.

As it is, I was totally distracted myself by a third figure in the room: a brooding, silent presence permeating the darkness of my bedroom and the interstices of my hyper-agile mind: Pius. When he saw what I was about, he became quite hysterical:

'You are completely insane, Mary Agnes. I had warned you, hadn't I? You think I can't see you and what you are up to? First you pretend you can't remember what you fed me while I was still alive and bedridden. And now, to top it all, you will have me witness your absurd gymnastic stunts?'

Initially, I ignored his apoplectic rage, but he had spoiled the occasion for me quite decisively. I couldn't turn my attention once more to the young man whose fervent caresses had ceased to stimulate me. But in the end I was glad I hadn't let him proceed further.

It didn't take long for him to lose interest himself.

I offered him something to eat, but he said he wasn't hungry. A drink? I have some brandy. But he wasn't thirsty either.

Stealthily, under cover of darkness, Sudarshan sneaked away from the advancing somnolence and mist of Daeva Danam.

For a while, I sat alone on a stone bench under the night sky. It was breezy and very cool, a slightly misshapen half-moon appeared and disappeared behind masses of swift-moving clouds.

And suddenly, apropos of nothing, scriptural verses I may have once been familiar with floated to my mind's surface like dregs of waterlogged scum.

'Add thou not unto His words, lest He reprove thee, and thou be found a liar.... If any man shall add unto the things of this book, God shall add unto him the plagues that are written in there.'

Could I have been hallucinating when I believed I was hearing the Voice of Jesus? Was some harsh punishment in store for me instead of the favoured treatment I believed I should be receiving?

An icy chill coursed through my body, making me shudder violently.

17

When I woke up next morning, I had forgotten all about the previous evening.

My first and only thought was: Today, I must deal with Thomachen, no matter what.

Why did I feel like punishing an old family retainer?

That's something I'm not easily able to analyse. But I sensed, unmistakably, that my intentions were entirely sadistic.

A light breakfast of tea and buttered toast after which I walked towards the spice garden and found Thomachen already there, waiting for me.

'Good morning, madam,' he called out nervously.

I chose not to return his greeting; instead, answered sourly, 'You don't fancy putting on your specs, do you? Thomachen!'

'Madam? Sorry, madam?'

'Your spectacles.... Do you never use them?'

'Oh, madam, the number has *changed* once again, I am thinking. Not able to see very much even with my spectacles on. Why, madam?'

'I should have known I can't trust you to alert me.... Thrips!'

'Pardon—Madam?'

I didn't repeat what I had said: even the first time I spoke the word it had been under my breath, in a deliberately venomous murmur. Now I marched him in silence to a patch of cardamom shrubs whose leaves showed the faint, preliminary signs of infestation: a latticework of puncturing and sucking that had created tiny contusions in leaf tissue.

I had happened to notice it only by chance, on the morning of my lunch with Sudarshan. Now I threw the news of this calamity at Thomachen like a whiplash.

It *was* a serious matter needing immediate redressal, certainly. But why was I picking on the old man, and in this menacing fashion? I should have been equally or more annoyed with Peter, who hadn't brought it to my attention either.

But Thomachen's spectacles were firmly perched on his beak-like nose now, and he was peering intently at every leaf contritely.

'Oh my God, look at that...just look at that, madam...ah, I see, I see.... You are so absolutely right, madam, it's thrips, definitely,' he confirmed. 'I didn't see it. I am so sorry. Luckily, it's still in the early stage.... Ah! What terrible plant disease this is. We caught it early, luckily....'

'No thanks to you, Thomachen.'

'No madam, I'm so sorry. But every thanks to you.... Fact is no one ever sees those sly buggers. Not a glimpse of them. They live in soil and come out only after dark, to suck up juice from the leaves.'

'Yes, yes. I know all that,' I snapped at him. 'But what are you going to do about it?'

'I know! I know what to do,' he said with evident excitement. 'Five or six bottles of Tholidol are in that shed. I will smear every leaf with the medicine!'

'Please. Those bottles are at least five or six years old. Just throw them out. And ask Peter to order half a dozen four-litre fresh jars of Tholidol urgently. Both of you must spray the shrubs thoroughly. And the soil too, in all affected patches...I don't want this to spread.'

'Yes madam, yes madam. Right now I will tell him,' he declared with unusual animation, and walked away purposefully to find Peter.

But soon, I believe that very next afternoon, a monstrous cloud of despair usurped the sky, swallowing every speck of light, every ounce of hope.

What the hell is happening; to me, to my world? The wonderment my home state inspires in all who encounter its quiet beauties has never before been tainted by such vicious irony.

God's own country—an advertising slogan that attracts millions to our shores every year—has turned into fetid swamp: wretched turbulence froths and ferments hour upon hour, day by day, while sheets of black rain batter the earth uninterruptedly.

Mountainous declivities here in Idukki have prevented any major flooding, but everywhere else Kerala is inundated. Torrential downpours have ruptured stately houses, pulverized humbler dwellings; entire farms are submerged and livelihoods decimated, bloated livestock, even human carcasses carried miles on raging waterways. And yet the rains continue to pound the earth. Is despotic climate change convulsing the globe faster than doomsayers had predicted? Are polar ice caps already liquefying, sea levels rising?

Are the end times upon us in this very hour?

Ominously destructive waves crash on our shores. Towering billows, punishing breakers augur the terrors of tsunami. The very earth seems to have tilted, tottering even as it whirls—a half-blinded, bloodied pugilist reeling in the ring under ceaseless blows from an unfairly heavier opponent.

Is it time, Jesus? Has the nightmare begun? Are the world's

billions about to be clasped in the rigor mortis of a final embrace?

∽

But simultaneously, stranger things had begun to happen to my personal life.

For one, Jesus hadn't spoken to me in days.

Something else too, difficult to explain: headaches, such as I've never before been prone to, excruciating and fairly immune to aspirin or paracetamol.

As soon as the weather lets up, I must go see a doctor.

Meanwhile, excessive rains have squelched any chance of a healthy spice crop this year. Perpetually overcast skies, combining with frigid temperatures engender terrible gloom and despair.

Even so, Thomachen has hardly absented himself for a single day. No matter how inclement the weather, he reports for work every morning at nine; and the spraying of Tholidol with a compressor gun on our routinely soggy cardamom shrubs commences. It's a daily regimen that's shared by him and Peter, morning and evening.

Despite the air of diluvial dreariness on the farm, the old man has found an unlikely but loyal friend in Nirmala. They are often together in their spare moments.

Once, I spied them sitting across each other in the old shed that Pius had converted into his workroom, chatting convivially and taking their lunch. Why did that sight inspire a flush of unreasoned anger in me?

Even more uncharitable thoughts flashed in my mind presently: can't she find a better way to spend her lunch break? Has she become so comfortable in the company of old men that she seeks to allure this one even older than Pius?

But no: that one glimpse of them should have made it more

than clear to me that Nirmala felt for this aged man much respect and empathy as she would have for her own father.

Soon after the bad spell of heavy rain, we had a whole week of sunny days. And the monkeys returned. There were two consecutive raids on our cardamom patch!

Now Thomachen, making amends for his oversight of the thrips affliction, assured me that he knew a trick or two that would ensure our simian cousins never returned to destroy our chances of reaping a fresh cardamom crop.

Early next morning I saw him using a stepladder to reach the highest stem of every cardamom bush in our garden. Tying little plastic bags to the main extruding branches with a string, each loaded with a spoonful of red powder, next he tied an identical pouch to lower stems. Soon every bush in the cardamom garden began to resemble a nursery of festooned Christmas trees!

'Chilli powder,' grinned Thomachen, when he had finished adorning the clumps. 'Monkeys always on prowl for tasty tidbits, by habit they never eat a morsel without first smelling, and then smearing it on their backsides! Always, that's an instinctual habit. A nice surprise awaits them when they tear open this attractive-looking fruit.'

Sure enough it happened almost exactly the way he had predicted: not the very next day, but after what may have been three or four, the precious hush of early morning was cleaved by terrible caterwauling, howls of outrage and grief—but presently, in less than a minute the cries of the monkeys diminished in their chaotic stridency, and then they were never seen or heard again on Daeva Danam!

Thomachen of course had not been present so early in the morning to derive any satisfaction from the success of his stratagem, but I told him about it, and he was pleased that his vast experience with cardamom-growing had finally proved to be of some use to our spice garden.

In less than a week, though, a tragic event occurred that submerged Daeva Danam in fresh and greater despondency.

It was Nirmala who discovered his body one morning, after the first farm workers had begun to arrive.

He was stretched out on the floor of Pius's old shed—face and body muscles horribly contorted and still.

When she found him, Nirmala raised an alarm; once other workers had rushed to the spot, she commenced a soft, ritual keening.

Thomachen was probably still alive at the time, although comatose. Peter tried unsuccessfully to contact an ambulance, but phone lines were down and the one vehicle that is stationed at the local hospital, ten kilometres away, was reportedly out of commission.

Clearly he had consumed a bottle of Tholidol after dark and spent the night on the premises without anyone's knowledge, secretly and silently suffering the excruciating torments of internal corrosion all by himself in Pius's workroom. Why?

Undoubtedly it may be mystificatory to speculate along these lines, but Nirmala's plaintive grieving put me in mind of the howling, outraged monkeys. Could they have cursed the architect of their grief so savagely as to drive him to take his own life?

Soon it became evident to all of us that no emergency services would be able to revive Thomachen. Nor could we uncover with any certainty the reason for his senseless act of self-destruction.

Many weeks later I was visited by a daughter of his, an only child who I knew had been estranged from him. They had heard about Thomachen's demise, but it didn't seem to affect them very much. Newly-wed, she came to Daeva Danam along with her husband, presumably to introduce him, and possibly with the expectation of receiving some sort of wedding gift. I gave her a crisp 500-rupee note in an ordinary white envelope on which I had scribbled 'Best Wishes'.

Her husband turned out to be the very same cousin who had once laid claim to Thomachen's two-acre plot in Parippu; through marriage, it had now become legally his.

Nirmala's grief on the occasion of Thomachen's death had been palpable.

Her pivotal role in Pius's poisoning hadn't caused her any apparent remorse, but when her older friend took his own life, her sorrow came pouring out.

That evening, I did feel ill at ease, and asked myself: had I persecuted the man so mercilessly as to drive him to suicide?

But I couldn't honestly believe that—after the first morning when I gave him a dressing-down for not reporting the outbreak of thrips, I had made it up with him; assuring him that in any case, this crop of cardamom would have been ruined by excessive rain.

Something else may have been bothering Thomachen which he hadn't revealed to anyone.

Nirmala gave me a possible clue to what it might be: apparently one night almost two years ago, when he had returned to Daeva Danam very late from his village, Thomachen had chanced upon Pius and Nirmala together.

Did he surprise them in a moment of intimacy? Was it tacit threat of blackmail that had persuaded Pius to change his mind about reinstating Thomachen?

After he passed away, Thomachen always claimed—as though it were some badge of honour or personal merit—great reverence and constant prayerful communication with my late husband.

Could he have been racked by a sense of guilt to take his own life? If indeed he had been blackmailing Pius?

No theory about Thomachen's suicide seemed adequate to disentangle the clump of loose threads surrounding it.

Shortly after his death, Nirmala left Daeva Danam.

A few weekends ago, she had visited the convent where Parvati had been raised; she went there with Peter and Parvati—a place called Hermitage of Sister Assunta in Kodikulam. Here, it would seem she had received an impromptu offer to join the nuns as trainee social worker for an outreach programme they were in the process of initiating. Nirmala herself may have indicated somehow to the nuns that she was looking for a change.

She begged me to excuse her, explaining that she strongly felt the need to engage in more useful and satisfying work.

Even before Nirmala went away, her cousin Chandrika whose mother had passed several months ago, decided that her place was in Edavani where she would look after and keep house for her ageing father.

My headaches have become less frequent. I have decided I should just ignore them, and perhaps they'll stop altogether?

18

As if to distract me from a jumble of nightmarish and disruptive events—the seemingly endless bouts of rain had fully abated days ago—a quiet Sunday morning begins for me with six consecutively mystifying phone calls from people I haven't spoken to in months.

My only kinship with these callers—if I can call it that at all—was that at one time, more than a year ago, they were all so-to-speak 'active' members, admirers and respectful fellow-worshippers, of my deceased husband's former parish and ministry.

Only days after he passed, some of these very people had proposed I take up the mantle and continue 'his good work'.

But in what way exactly do you mean?

To start with, a Bible studies class? We could meet twice a week at your place—Daeva Danam is so convenient and accessible, what better tribute can we pay the Pastor than to further his legacy and follow in his footsteps?

In fact, one of their women, whose husband owned a bakery, offered to provide free refreshment—cake and coffee, gratis—for every Bible study meeting we held!

Unable to feel quite so sanguine myself about Pius's 'legacy' I had remained noncommittal, pleading that I just wasn't learned or eloquent enough to conduct such meetings; besides, of course, being still too saddened and disorientated by my husband's passing.

In the meanwhile the first run of Pius's sermons—a relatively slim booklet—had already sold out, and there had been talk of another edition in coming days; but after that no mention of it at all.

Then surprisingly this Sunday morning a chorus of practically the same busybodies chanting in unison that I shouldn't be shy of sharing my 'wisdom' with the community—wisdom?—my thoughts, sermons, messages from the beyond: if nothing else, one of them reiterated, we could revive that old idea, never acted upon, of a Bible study class, to have better grasp on the host of predictions divulged in the Good Book!

Utterly bewildered, my hackles rose nevertheless with clammy suspicion at the mention of 'messages from beyond', but not until later that morning, when Parveen came over, as she had promised she would, did I unscramble the puzzle of those serial, copycat phone calls.

I don't know it then, but in her handbag Parveen had brought along that Sunday's edition of *The Clarion* which featured a full-page spread of an article written by one R. Sudarshan that had caught Parveen's attention.

But before she showed it to me, other more pressing information took precedence—terribly excited, but worried and disheartened too, she told me that her younger boy, Jamsheed, was back from Syria!

I was myself excited to hear that.

But breathlessly, she went on to tell me that he was being held by the NIA: the National Intelligence Agency, which had arrested him as soon he disembarked at Cochin airport.

Charging him with sedition for having joined the so-called Islamic State and fought, however briefly, in their ranks, he had been allowed just one phone call to his family. But later, she said, she had received yet another call from an officer of the same agency saying they would hold Jamshed for an unspecified period of time to question him about his elder brother, who hadn't come back—although they had left India together.

Poor Parveen was obviously very disturbed.

'Rumi was terribly unforgiving when Jamsheed said he wanted to go back home,' she said, 'calling him a baby and more vicious names as well, the biggest mistake of my life he said, to agree to let you come along. As you probably remember, Jamsheed was always the gentler of the two, it didn't take long for him to decide, within three months of being with the militants, he didn't like their brutal ways at all.

'The brothers had quarrelled bitterly, but at least thank heavens, Rumi didn't betray him…so Jamsheed managed to slip away one night, while Rumi—that ass was always rebellious—has decided to stay on and fight, for the Caliphate, if you please! Can you believe it? Can you? I still can't…. By the way, have you heard at all from Mark?'

I didn't answer, and she realized she needn't have asked.

But to an extent she was happy, at least one of her sons, though incarcerated at present, was back in the country and safe.

I offered her coffee, which at first she refused; but only moments later remembering the newspaper in her handbag she extricated a neatly folded miniature rectangle.

'Oh, let me show you this…have you seen it?' she asked. 'It's from *The Clarion*'s Sunday magazine.'

'I switched to *Indian Express* years ago….'

'But no, you must read this piece…in today's *Clarion*.'

I looked at the banner headline on the creased paper she held out to me:

IN SEARCH OF THE FINAL PROPHET...

Below that, in bolder type, was the main title:

KOTTAYAM CASSANDRA CLAIMS HOTLINE TO GOD:

Prophesies End of the World!

'Take your time,' said Parveen. 'I'm going for a walk.... If Parvati's around shall I ask her to make you some coffee?'

'Sure, but have something yourself, why don't you...?'

'Maybe I will too. By the time you've finished with that article, I'll be back with coffee for both of us. Do share your guesses with me. Which of our neighbours do you think this could be about?'

Until I saw the byline, I didn't know he was an *R.* Sudarshan. Never had reason to enquire about his initials while we were getting drunk together, or I was allowing him—*provoking* him, possibly—to seduce me.... Was I? Probably not.

But then he hadn't mentioned to me that he was planning to write such a front-page exposé based on our private conversations over lunch at the Marina!

Flashes of remembrance, pontificatory effusions, jagged shards of a bizarre afternoon and evening impinged on my memory. I felt awful: sheepish, and also aghast.

At first I scoured through the article quickly, just to see if... no, thank heavens my name didn't seem to figure anywhere.... And then I read his well-written copy once more, attentively.

The piece began with much fanfare: he described an extraordinary website that had created a sensation among internet users all over the world in which the author—somebody who called himself (or herself) TheLastProphet.com—had claimed that

Jesus had been dictating messages to him or her for dissemination to the world at large!

As might be expected, this had caused something of a frisson—no, tidal waves of excitement—especially among the fundamentalist Pentecostal community of the Christian world. The reporter first gave a gist of five posts that had already appeared on the portal.

Now there was a digression of a slightly technical nature which detailed advancements in computer science that had made it possible to zero in on the approximate geographical vertices of a website's domain and trace its origins.

The World Wide Web, lamented Sudarshan, had, in this way, perhaps lost some of its enticing anonymity, a source of so much satisfaction and charm to its users until recently; but on the other hand, it had made it possible for him to track down 'The Last Prophet'.

He gave details (including price) of a device called 'Eye Spy' which he himself had made use of to successfully locate the regional seat of TheLastProphet.com.

Contrary to his own expectations, he had found that this website emanated from a district called Idukki in southwest Kerala, a hilly spice-growing region, not so far from the nodal towns of Kottayam and Kanjirappally, both strongholds of the Syrian Christian community of Kerala that boasted of large farmhouses producing quantities of rice, coconut, rubber and spice.

Incidentally, the article went on to say, Idukki was also home to one of the most illustrious pastors of the Evangelist movement in Kerala, the late Pius Pascal Philipose, who had passed away barely a year ago.

There you have it. Short of naming me, Sudarshan had spared himself no pains to indicate to local denizens of the region between Thekaddy and Kanjirappally—my home stretch—who the mystery Last Prophet could possibly be.

And there, too, you had the probable reason for that morning's chain of mysterious phone calls—people acquainted with me who had been seized with a powerful hunch—without indicating as much—about The Last Prophet's identity! How excited they must feel that they had by simple inference and logical deduction legitimately hit upon so vast and celestial a secret!

How much, I wondered, would Sudarshan have been paid by *The Clarion* for doing this investigation and for writing this sensational piece? Three or four thousand rupees? Maybe five thousand at most?

Was that all getting to know me—making that cavalier bid to seduce me, besides—been worth?

And I was glad, wasn't I, that I had had the sense to firmly put a stop to his sexual advances when he had tried to press further?

Of course, he had made sure to insist on paying the entire bill—some three-and-a-half thousand rupees—for lunch and drinks at the Marina: during which repast, with simpering hypocrisy, he had ferreted out my views on Biblical eschatology and the future of the world—all towards providing copy and ballast for the findings of his tracking device!

And fool that I was I had trusted him so completely, even during his first visit to my place in the company of the new pastor.

I found myself increasingly depressed as I read through his piece: it stung my heart and entirely anaesthetized me.

I avoided mentioning to Parveen that I knew and had spent an entire afternooon with the author of the piece she had just shown me. Luckily, she didn't stay very long after coffee, and perhaps sensed I wasn't in the mood for conversation.

After he left Daeva Danam that evening at dusk, Sudarshan

hadn't phoned me, let alone mention that a tell-all report such as the one I had just seen would be in print within days.

In fact, he had never mentioned his journalism to me at all through the course of that afternoon, although his byline in *The Clarion* described him as 'a prolific freelancer'.

I waited five whole days before tentatively dialling a cell number he had given me, but it only rang. I tried again that evening and heard a recorded message which intoned, in a strangely mechanical voice,

'This number does not exist!'

Perhaps smart new phones allow you to play back such messages to shrug off unwanted callers?

Or could he be travelling again following another exciting story, and had simply lost interest in the last one?

The following Sunday—I made it a point to remember to tell my newspaper vendor to leave for me *The Clarion* as well—I read a news report in the tabloid by someone called Aneesh P. that told the story of an untouchable Dalit who had spent ten years behind bars as an undertrial in Bihar. His only offense—or misfortune, rather—had been allowing himself to be apprehended by a TC while travelling ticketless on a train to Patna. Never produced before a magistrate or court of law, he had been despairing of his fate ever since—until his and other similar cases were drawn to the attention of the Patna High Court, resulting in an order that he be set free!

Could something like that have happened to my son? God forbid, no. I was sure it hadn't. No, Mark had simply decided to reject his parents and his past completely; for some reason I couldn't help but feel certain that was the case.

As I mentioned before, I saw Sudarshan again one more time, and only for an instant.

The Prospect of Miracles

I was travelling in the back seat of our SUV being driven by Peter to Alleppey when I caught sight of him. Parvati was next to Peter in the front seat.

As we were leaving the outskirts of Kottayam, I caught a glimpse of Sudarshan, travelling in a public bus that had stalled at a traffic signal.

It was so brief a moment I could have been wrong, but I know I wasn't. Our eyes met: instantly he looked away, pretending he hadn't seen me.

∽

In the days before this sighting happened, however, I had myself been terribly preoccupied and simply agog with excitement.

For the most part I had stayed in my bedroom, with clear instructions to the servants that I was not to be disturbed.

The reason for my withdrawal and preferred seclusion was that once again I was receiving messages from Jesus at an unprecedented pace; and, in terms of content too, it was clearer to me that our time was running out—hence the urgency of their tenor; I could hear an unmistakable note of pleading in the beseeching despair of His appeals.

……Every abhorrent sin, every lustful exhibition is flaunted publicly in flagrant contempt of My Father.

He watches it all immersed in deep sorrow, even as His own children show no qualms about behaving like animals.

Only because of His Love for them—which overrides his grief—does He bother to chastise you. Remember this always. Never, never, even if His anger seems overwhelming at times, should you believe otherwise.

Only a very few—faithful followers of my last prophet—will surely be protected in the face of the unending horror soon to engulf the Earth.

So while I took dictation from the Lord with accuracy and diligence, the irony of my own delinquency—or call it appalling self-indulgence, if you please—didn't escape me. For the sake of lecherous, momentary pleasure—thirty pieces of silver, no less—I had practically betrayed our Lord once again.

What are we to do with you, Mary Agnes? Have you no shame at all?

How dreadful will be your punishment as you gloss over one mortal sin in your very recent past, and soon after titillate yourself—virtually succumbing to—another awful temptation?

But I didn't do it, did I? Sorely tempted my body may have been, but I stopped short of indulging it. Jesus, please do remember that when we meet. You must.

And all the time, my inner desperation was actually growing: headaches had started again. Loquacity ran on at full throttle in my head; but, afloat on a flimsy raft I felt as though choppy tides of historical inevitability were about to take me down.

Not just that.

Something else had gone seriously wrong with me. With my brain? Often, I found myself thinking of an urgent task I needed to follow up on, but just as I stepped out of my bedroom to attend to it, I had forgotten what it was I came out to do.

Last Sunday, for instance, I knew I had arranged to meet someone in town, but couldn't for the life of me remember who it was I had to meet, or where.

Unnerving it was to find myself becoming so forgetful. But I took a kindly view of these lapses of memory.

I said to myself, never mind, let me go into town anyway—I have some shopping to do, don't I? Perhaps by sheer accident

I'll run into the very person or persons I had planned to meet.

So I hailed an autorickshaw and asked the driver to take me to Erattupetta market.

I had lost all track of time, and didn't have any idea how long we had been moving, although there wasn't much traffic on the road, when suddenly I saw the front façade of the grand white shrine of St Thomas Mar Thoma Church.

'Stop! Stop...'

Abruptly, I asked the auto-driver to stop right there.

'Madam? Erattupetta market is still a long way off....'

'Yes,' I said to the auto driver rudely. 'And you've been taking me for a nice long ride. After going round and round, we're still back near my house from where we started! I'm a local person please, Chetta. Don't believe you can take me on a wild goose chase.'

The driver took offense at my insinuation. He started grumbling, breaking into Malayalam, in the end almost yelling at me.

'It's a no entry at that junction, madam. I have to take you round this way. There is no other way to catch the main road. I'm not cheating you. If you think so, you can find another auto.'

'Yes, that's just what I'm going to do,' I said, and paid him the minimum fare. He was most annoyed, grumbling about my ignorance of roads and traffic rules and when I got out, sped away.

Yes, this church is my church. The one I had been familiar with in childhood. It was, in fact, just a stone's throw from Daeva Danam. It was filled with people. Some ceremony was underway. Standing in its porch, I watched as two colourfully robed priests in white cassocks lined with red and gold brocade conducted a solemn mass, chanting in Aramaic.

Yes, this was the Syrian Christian faith I had abandoned

so many years ago to keep pace with Pius's eccentric beliefs. I felt deep regret that I had allowed myself to turn so pliant and submissive to his pet obsessions.

At peace now within the sanctuary of what I could call my family church, I felt as though, after a long and circuitous diversion I had finally made it home.

Roused from a deep reverie by a hoarse whisper, I started. 'Kochamma! After so long....'

I smiled at a thickset man, who looked vaguely familiar. Out of sheer politeness. He was practically bald with a long beard of dense curls, but in the end I couldn't place him at all.

Presently, I climbed back into another auto and proceeded on my way; made random purchases for my kitchen in Erattupetta, then went back home in the same autorickshaw.

No sooner had I reached home I felt my headache coming on, and swallowed two Crocin tablets that had no effect at all.

19

A whole month after R. Sudarshan's article appeared in *The Clarion*, its disclosures seemed not to hold any direct consequence for me; at least, none I could perceive—apart from that rosary of Sunday morning phone calls.

However, without my knowledge a great divertissement of speculative fervour had been set in motion—privately, inside the homes of core Pentecostal followers who had read and pondered Sudarshan's piece: intrigues, debates, guessing games, powwows all received full-blown stimulus.

While Sudarshan's journalistic crystal-gazing augmented for some their worst fears of the imminence of end times, others found their most ardent hopes about Jesus's Second Coming burgeoning to full bloom: the topical relevance of this cleverly appealing piece was further intensified by the coincidence of a series of unprecedented natural and man-made disasters.

∽

A landslide in a remote corner of Himachal had claimed an entire village of 300, with only a handful of maimed survivors.

Sixty migrant tea plantation workers had been massacred by gunmen belonging to a contentious caste-primacy group which claimed that given rampant unemployment among local

Assamese youth these outsiders had no place in the state.

Chennai, at the other end of the country, was submerged by heavy rain—the city's main avenues, by-lanes, highways inundated—and dozens, it was reported, fell into open manholes and drowned; it was a catastrophe which the city's oldest residents couldn't recall any equivalence to.

Predictably, the city's Met department had woefully little to say—except that this was the worst flooding to have taken place in a hundred and forty years; which happened to be approximately the very time when official documenting of weather records willy-nilly began. Few journalists were perceptive enough to blame the calamity on the municipal corporation, whose venal councillors had permitted indiscriminate building activity, blocking natural waterways, choking mangroves and rainwater egress.

In other parts of the world too—Australia, Portugal, California—there were unprecedented forest fires raging for weeks on end, proving almost impossible to quench; at the same time that some Indonesian islands were reeling under a tsunami.

And then when it had gathered public momentum, panic swept through Kanjirappally, Kottayam, and indeed many subdivisions of Idukki as well—places where Kerala's Christian population resided—like a raging whirlwind.

༄

A coterie of core loyalists of our Pentecostal church had already worked out a plan of action—my concurrence to it taken as fait accompli—on the assumption that I wouldn't be averse to publicity on such an ostentatious scale, culminating in a grand public spiritual catharsis.

I first heard details of the plan when it was related to me at my home by Thomas Mathew and Manike Jiju, two elders of the

Pentecostal community. They had underscored the fact that it had already been discussed by their committee with Pastor Perambil, who had given it an unreserved thumbs-up—besides promising financial assistance to cover the high incidental costs such as hiring of a large open-air stadium for one evening, printing of posters, handbills, etc.

For a few minutes, to be honest, I was seriously annoyed by the extent of their presumption: surely they should have checked with me first, if I was really the internet lady as surmised by some readers of the piece in *The Clarion*, and if I would in fact be willing to take on all they had envisaged?

⁓

The simple argument in favour of excluding me from the nitty-gritties of permissions and preparations was based on their utmost confidence that I would never decline: after all their proposal was no more than an elaborate stratagem to achieve the Lord's own objectives more effectively.

In the end, they were right: I wasn't able to resist any of it I mean—being described as a Prophet of the Lord on large colourful hoardings and posters that came up overnight everywhere in the city. Where had they got hold of that picture—clicked at my engagement with Pius?—I looked demurely reticent in it, and much prettier than I can in reality claim to be.

But there were other misgivings I was harrowed by which I could hardly discuss with the organizers of this splendid religious fiesta: the truth was I was very concerned. If I counted the squares on the wall calendar for every date that had passed by since the last time the Lord spoke to me, I realized with sinking heart that once again He hadn't uttered a word to me in the last twenty days!

Not a whisper, or murmur, not a whiff of His fresh breath which I so longed for.

Was He annoyed? Would He disapprove of public shenanigans of the sort the Pentecostals had devised for me?

Lights, special effects, full page ads in local Malayalam newspapers?

My immediate problem though was that apart from my routine lapses of memory I was now suffering a more serious one: I just couldn't recollect, try hard as I did, if when He first spoke to me He hadn't cautioned against public fanfare, specifically urging me to remain anonymous, not take any personal credit for performing the task He was assigning me.

I had only a vague yet abiding impression that this had indeed been the case. No signature bows for myself Jesus had insisted, no self-aggrandizement of any sort: because all of this was primarily—and so obviously—a spiritual exercise towards glorifying and beseeching mercy from Father God!

Right through my fairly extensive discussions with members of the Pentecostal board, a persistent sentiment to this effect nagged me; yet, I am ashamed to say, I didn't once give it expression.

Wasn't that because my own grasp of this sine qua non had somehow degenerated into sloppy inexactitude—a decay surely engendered by fatuous vanity, my reluctance to forsake the pomp and grandeur associated with a self-endowed nomenclature? The wicked self-love of believing that since it was I who had been picked as His Last Prophet—and not by random choice—there *had* to be something uniquely special about me?

Lord Jesus *had* chosen me, in fact, hadn't He? About that there could be hardly any doubt.

Another part of my mind dismissed every misgiving and

uncertainty, arguing in tandem with the organizers of this grand Pentecostal jamboree: why would He be displeased? Hadn't this been His very design and intent when He chose me to transmit His admonitions to the world? There was no scope for ambivalence.

As Mathew and Jiju had rationalized when they came to see me on that very first occasion: only large-scale public events like this one had the potential for most effectively disseminating the Lord's Word throughout the world—print media taking over our task more comprehensively the following morning.

The committee of Pentecostals assured me they had in fact sent out invitations to several Indian as well as international news agencies, inviting reporters to cover the gala proceedings.

∽

Ah, fateful Friday! Would my life have turned out differently had I asked for the event to be shifted to a Sunday, my favourite day of the week?

But I remember there was an important football league engagement scheduled for that Sunday—and the stadium was fully booked for three consecutive weeks after that. So Friday, the twenty-seventh it was—I would have a whole week to prepare for all that I wished to declaim before a packed Nehru Stadium in central Kottayam.

The Pentecostals had gone the whole hog and hired a professional 'events manager' to ensure the evening's success: he brought in tow a lights-man, a sound engineer, as well as a caterer who would provide free tea and snacks to the audience; followed by a pricey dinner with an elaborate menu that was being offered to all those whose appetites had been sufficiently stimulated by the evening's fare.

Nevertheless, I remained anxious.

At full capacity, the stadium held about eighteen thousand people! I was not at all comfortable with the idea of speaking before such large audiences, but took solace in the fact that only a fraction of this massive throng might actually show up—after all I didn't I have the drawing power of the Kerala Blasters or some such popular football team—the powerful magnets that often galvanized this venue until it was bursting at the seams!

I was relieved to hear that my own discourse on messages I had received from God would be preceded by two introductory speakers: Pastor Perambil himself, and the bishop of our diocese, K. R. Joshua Paulose, an ailing and but enthusiastic priest seventy-nine years of age, who had decided to make an exceptional public appearance for this spectacular event.

Picked up by a chauffeur-driven limousine at 6.30 p.m., when I was brought to the venue that evening the stadium was ablaze with powerful floodlights; fifteen minutes to go, and people were still trickling in.

In the centre of the football field, under a colourful marquee, a large stage had been erected; and quite rapidly, three wings of the stands—the ones facing and flanking centre stage—were filled almost to capacity. Only one solitary wing of the stands remained unlit and unoccupied—the one behind the stage.

Here, under the staggered seating of the unused pavilion, a tiny press room had been improvised. I was requested to meet accredited journalists in this cubbyhole during the intermission which would last about forty-five minutes—more than enough time for the more determined members of the audience to avail of a free tomato-and-cucumber sandwich and a Styrofoam cup of steaming coffee; however, it had been made clear to me that I need answer only such questions as I was comfortable with.

As Manike Jiju a stately, landowning dowager with frizzy hair and pendant earrings had emphasized during our last meeting at Daeva Danam, 'I suspect this evening is going to turn up something quite sensational, Mary Agnes. Essentially a celebration of faith, but in the course of which we may well witness outpourings of emotion—both anguish and expectation, possibly spontaneous healings as well. Be prepared for miraculous manifestations, Mary Agnes. Hallelujah! Praise the Lord!'

But as I have mentioned earlier, I didn't have the confidence to reinforce her enthusiasm: the Lord hadn't spoken to me in quite a while.

I felt abandoned, painfully aware of the sickening reality that I had lost contact with my Saviour. I must have done something horribly wrong to have incurred such displeasure.

But there was this other voice, quite distinct that echoed horribly in my ears at times; mocking me, cackling, sometimes shrieking hysterically.

'So Mary Agnes,' at first I had assumed it was only Pius taking his usual potshots at me, 'so now you will have us believe you have become a high priestess of the Lord? A murderous bride-of-Christ? Hehe, hehe.'

But then, on the very eve of my function, as the clock struck midnight and I struggled in flushed anticipation to catch some sleep, this same other voice rang out loud, deafeningly loud: stripped of every obfuscation or dissimulating overtone, painfully strident in its weirdly chilling modulation.

With horror I realized that, without a doubt, this was not the Lord who was speaking, but the Evil One who had decided it was time to focus his attentions on me.

No. Oh no, no...

Much too disturbed by a sleepless night to be able to make any credible sense of what Pastor Perambil or, for that matter the bishop, were droning on about, I sat there waiting, backstage. As at all public events, the chief guests were unable to arrive at any reasonable estimate of how long they should hold the podium.

At last it was my turn to address the dignified but now restless hordes.

Feeling terribly hot, with perspiration pouring down my face, my eyes dazzled by lights, a fierce applause exploded when I walked up to the mike.

I don't remember very much of what I said that evening. I believe I managed only a very few words....

'My dear friends...fellow-believers.... The Lord has been kind.... At the eleventh hour, in His Infinite Mercy, He has given us a last chance to repent....'

And then it began.

The entire public address system seemed to go into overdrive: deafeningly loud feedback, shrill aural distortion, shrieking hysteria, ululating yawls that could put the fear of the Beast into every living creature within earshot.

All of this made me giddy and nauseous.

The whole stage began to rotate: first slowly, like a carousel commencing its mindless circuitous orbit at a fairground, then faster, faster...even faster...suddenly: anti-clockwise—in reverse!

∽

Later when they came to see me in hospital, Thomas Mathew and Manike Jiju said, 'A tremendous roar of approval went up in the stadium as soon as you got on stage.... And then when you collapsed, believers were convinced you had been "slain in the spirit", the way special souls becomes possessed by the Holy Spirit. Your body began to twitch, as though in an epileptic fit. There was tremendous applause when that happened as well.... It was as if, no matter what, the public was determined to enjoy a fruitful confirmation of their evening's hopes....

'But a few minutes later, some of our volunteers realized all wasn't well, we rushed onto stage to help revive you. Fortunately, one of our committee, Dr Namputhri, the well-known neurologist, was standing by and insisted on your being immediately moved to his private nursing home. It was then we saw the trickle of blood that had stained your lips...even though your eyes were open but unseeing.

'After you were carried away, we made several announcements about the unforeseen and abrupt end to the evening's function, but many of the public showed their displeasure by booing and insisting on the promised tea and snacks. Some riff-raff had got in along with the genuine audience...they made a bonfire of the detachable folding chairs and the fire brigade had to be summoned.'

20

To begin with, highly qualified doctors at a new super-specialty hospital on Vypin Island (which Dr Namputhri himself had recommended she be shifted to) agreed that what Mary Agnes had suffered was a severe nervous breakdown.

Her every symptom seemed to corroborate this. Right away, she was put on a regimen of anti-depressants and a strong nightly dose of barbital.

But extraordinarily, on her third morning there, she was woken up very early and bundled onto the ward's gurney—nil by mouth—then launched bleary-eyed on a swift-moving almost psychedelic journey through a maze of vacuous corridors, low, sometimes dazzling lights, precipitous corners, unexpected clutter, noise, crowds, colour, silence, then deserted passages again, and finally through mirror-like swivel doors of an ultrasound laboratory.

Possibly, an incompetent nurse or ward boy misread the bed number the matron had scribbled on her requisition form, thus subjecting her to a complete CT scan, which was in fact intended for a cancer survivor (fast asleep in the curtained other half of the same room).

The scan however proved timely, a fortuitous error which revealed a swollen aneurism in her hypothalamus that required emergency intervention.

Performed post-haste by a team of ace surgeons, the operation was deemed a complete success. The doctors congratulated themselves on saving a patient's life in the nick of time, but once she came through—head shaven, swaddled in bandages—the primary prognosis was further reconfirmed through intensive psychological and clinical testing; and her morbidity perceived not to have improved at all, possibly further deteriorated.

In retrospect, Mary Agnes was able to narrate these events as if at the time they were happening she had an objective awareness and grasp of what she was being put through. In reality, of course, that was not the case. When she was not anaesthetized and unconscious, she was sedated, and the entire experience of those six-and-a-half weeks in hospital had been disjointed, unfolding more as dream-like phantasmagoria.

One week in intensive care during much of which she was only partly conscious, followed by five-and-a-half tedious weeks in a now independent room, and she was deemed by doctors to have sufficiently recovered from her brain surgery.

But all told, this was a bleak and difficult passage for her.

On the one hand, recovery from surgical trauma was slow and arduous, following the same gradual process of healing as it would in the normal course of things; on the other hand, she was suffering from a bleak and terrible sense of loss.

The Voice of our Lord which she had grown so used to hearing, and which had become a great solace to her, had not spoken again. It had dried up completely in the last eight weeks. Drugs she was being given on a regular basis rendered her passive, sullen and inactive.

Nevertheless, she was discharged from the island's bustling health centre to make room for a crush of new patients, and of course, this itself brought about a lively change in her—she was delighted to be going home again.

A few days later she was back at Daeva Danam, having travelled in the company of Peter and Parvati. Acting on an informal appeal by a group of parishioners, friends of the community and the pastor himself, they had consented to assume greater responsibility in the running of the plantation and guardianship of their ailing mistress: they had moved in lock, stock, and barrel at the farm.

Another piece of good news which she heard directly from Pastor Perambil when he visited her at hospital just before she was discharged: Pius's lawyers had explicitly asked him to convey to 'Madam' that she need have no financial worries for the immediate future. Pastor Philipose, apart from everything else he achieved in his florid life, had squirrelled away a considerable amount of money which now, with legal procedures complete, had been credited to Mary Agnes's bank account.

Once back at home, she felt she was making progress day by day. She was feeling pretty good within herself.

This peaceful interlude was violently disrupted one evening—when she was told about the incident later, she could barely remember it, let alone explain or justify it—Mary Agnes attacked Peter with a kitchen knife, was restrained by Parvati in the nick of time, and disarmed.

All three of them happened to be in the kitchen together. Parvati was cooking a vegetable curry for Mary on the gas stove; then she turned the gas off and went into the yard to fetch some fresh tamarind to add to her curry.

The whole incident probably had its inception during their car ride from Vypin to Daeva Danam. Peter was at the wheel, his wife next to him in front, and Mary Agnes had the back seat all to herself.

After she had travelled for a while she noticed how often Peter kept glancing at her, even making eye contact, in the rear-view mirror. Now per se she knew that he was a good driver, so she could hardly reprimand him to keep his eyes on the road. But his interest in her made Mary distinctly uncomfortable. Once or twice she caught the flicker of a smile on his lips; at another time, he blinked pointedly at her—with both eyes.

When they had reached home soon after, she was too delighted by the beauties she witnessed once again and had no reason to bring up the subject with him. But over the next few days she repeatedly suspected that he had developed an unusual interest in her. Had he classified her in his mind as a 'mental case', thus helpless, and easy prey for his own wayward, salacious impulses?

But, the chaotic surge of feelings that besieged her mind every time she observed—or assumed—Peter's peculiar interest in her, had in fact a greater bearing on the silly man's wife: poor Parvati, Mary was brooding, how fickle and capricious men can be towards their life partners.

So that evening, when Parvati had gone into the garden to fetch tamarind, and Mary was leaning over the tureen that held the freshly-made curry, taking its aroma, Peter had brushed against her protruding rump in a rather deliberate and familiar manner—or so it had seemed to her. Mary lost her temper and picked up a knife lying on the kitchen platform she was bending over. Luckily, Parvati came back just in time and wrestled it out of her fierce grip.

Doctors described her bout of rage as an 'unfortunate relapse'. Nevertheless, once her anger and anguish subsided she became peaceable again; but at the advice of several doctors and with her consent, she agreed to shift to another reputed establishment run by nuns of The Order of Sister Sophia and the Sacred Sacrament that nestled on the backwaters of Alleppey.

While in the throes of relapse her medication had been stepped up, but finally tapered down to what doctors call a 'maintenance' dose, and she was considered well enough to move to the home in Alleppey.

∽

A very silent and scenic estate named rather dauntingly Ashram for the Mentally Afflicted.

But compassion and sensibility were the mainspring of the Italian sisters' approach to succouring patients, which revived their sense of mental well-being, not just through rudimentary healthcare as at a hospice, but also by inculcating habits of Christian piety and prayer. The sisters believed they had seen proof of the love of Jesus, how decent living habits anchored the innermost affective passions of the dysfunctional when aided by salutary routine, the endowments of chastity and moral rectitude.

Early morning mass at a small chapel in the main building, followed by half-an-hour of hymn-singing led by Sister Esmerelda who accompanied them on her portable electric organ; group physical exercises conducted by Sister Benito shortly after and voluntary kitchen service under the supervision of Sister Bice, besides a systematic dusting of lounge furniture, sweeping and swabbing of living room and dormitories—these were some of the activities that kept patients and sisters busy all day long, the sisters cheerfully participating in every chore while keeping an eye on their wards; followed by an optional evening service in the chapel.

A somewhat hectic routine, but most patients were more than happy to stay active; many, it was true, remained slumped in depression through many hours of day, while a few became frantically hyperactive at times. But something about the peaceful surroundings appeared to have a definitely calming effect on the afflicted, though there were others too whom it may have rendered irritable or torpid.

A good-looking, middle-aged priest called Fr Roberto Quinto, permanently rostered in the small, not-too-distant enclave of Champakulam visited them every Sunday to celebrate mass. He seemed to enjoy his visits to Alleppey and the Ashram so much that very often he prolonged his sojourn by a couple of days, just to remain a little longer on the tranquil estate. Often, he spent time counselling patients in a most homely, down-to-earth manner.

Day-to-day tasks and obligations, central to the sisters' way of life, encouraged inmates to assume responsibility—cooking and cleaning, group prayer and discussion—all of these the sisters believed were instrumental in enabling patients to feel normal and find healing; although, it was also a fact that very few inmates left the home once they had become a part of it to resume normal social life.

Before she had joined the Order some twenty-seven years ago, and later took charge of the Ashram in Alleppey, Mother Superior Clarissa Corda, brain behind this ameliorative endeavour, had worked as a psychologist in Rome training batches of young nuns for the contemplative life and service to the poor.

Of course, not all inmates at the Ashram were financially disadvantaged, although it was true that most were elderly.

Mary Agnes, a lot more sophisticated in education and upbringing than the slightly wretched common folk who made up most of the Ashram's forty-odd residential inmates, was granted no special favours or facilities—a small donation made at the suggestion of Pastor Perambil just a few days before joining the retreat notwithstanding,

She slept in a common dormitory shared by five other recovering patients, and during her two 'free' hours every evening spent a great deal of time in silent prayer at the chapel, sometimes alongside others.

Jasper, an old retainer who had been with them for seventeen of the eighteen years the home had been in existence made trips to town once or twice a week whenever additional purchases or official paperwork demanded it. Vegetables, fruits and other provisions were regularly supplied by boat to the Ashram which had its own private landing pier.

Occasional crumbly bits of inmates' sorrows and torments floated to her ears: a few sank in as though by way of some osmotic relay, but left hardly any lasting impression at all: a middle-aged mother, Alphonse, had choked her infant son to death while feeding him gruel because of her obsession with fattening an underweight baby: she had continued to stuff his mouth with semi-solids, not realizing that he was gasping for breath. To this day she enacted a mournful, nightly ritual of feeding, burping and tucking an imaginary infant into bed before flopping into a densely comatose inertia herself that no mortal agency could easily disturb.

A middle-aged barber by the name of Gonzalo Nambiar, whose own overgrown and patchy tufts of hair were styled in a most bizarre fashion, was utterly convinced that nuns at their institution pretended to Roman Catholicism, but in fact were bonded in a conspiracy to practise black magic rites; that Fr Roberto himself, when he visited the Ashram every Sunday, solemnized a dastardly black mass. Gonzalo buttonholed every patient or orderly he met through the course of the day, whispering his suspicions urgently in their ears.

A former trapeze artiste with the unusual professional name of Flying Koel had been sexually abused as a young boy by his ringmaster for years. The circus had closed sometime in the remote past—he was himself an old man now—yet to this day he trod gingerly along perpendiculars delineated by the solid marble slabs of the floor imagining he was walking a tightrope high in the air, complaining all the while about daredevil acts he needed to perform even at his age, without so much as a safety net beneath!

Nevertheless, details of these fragmented lives heard sometimes from patients themselves, and sometimes from their admirers and friends, were so mutative and fanciful Mary Agnes failed to sustain any genuine feeling for the grief they presumably camouflaged.

A number of inmates were too perplexed or self-absorbed to notice anything at all, muttering and cursing to eternal perdition a range of dramatis personae drawn from the psychic firmament of what might well have been a lifetime, or perhaps several past ones. Others muttered obscenities under their breath, detailing sexual outrages committed by unknown persons on their near and dear ones in defiance of all measure of decency; but sheer repetition made this lot sound as though they deeply relished what they so abhorred.

There were also a few inmates who believed the worst was over, that they had completely recovered from a brief illness and were soon to be going back home—although where that home was, or who was waiting there to welcome them back—remained entirely nebulous.

Hardly aware at first of her feelings, Mary Agnes was drawn, inevitably, to the priest who came there every Sunday to celebrate mass: she made it a point never to miss confession with Fr Roberto—despite several dire warnings from Gonzalo that he was not the person he pretended to be.

In the vagaries of her daydreams she fantasized that the priest and she shared a special affinity.

She would prolong her confessional sessions with him as much as possible, often rambling into anecdotes of her life with Pastor Philipose, which the sedentary and possibly disinterested Father heard out in noncommittal silence. She always preferred to begin her own session only after other supplicants had finished and left the chapel, so he could give her enough time.

These stories tended rather flaccidly towards make-believe, harking romantically back to Pius's early days of courtship, and the time when Mark was still very much a child. If the priest felt impatient with her meanderings, he did not protest—except perhaps in assigning her an excessive number of Hail Marys to recite by way of penance.

So she began to believe that he enjoyed listening to her stories as much as she did recounting them; although once or twice she had reason to wonder if that wasn't a soft snore she heard from behind the latticed screen of the confessional window during her digressive monologues?

And then, one Sunday, while kneeling before the confessional she broke down and sobbed bitterly. She couldn't stop crying.

At first, Fr Roberto waited patiently for her to compose herself. But her sobs only grew more staccato and strangulated. The priest spoke, 'What's troubling you, my child? You can tell me anything.'

'For many months I believed Jesus had chosen me His messenger....'

Here she was overwhelmed again.

'Yes, for the longest time I imagined we shared a special relationship.... He loved me, Jesus, I could feel that.'

'He still does, you can be sure,' murmured the priest.

'Then one day Satan put this thought in my head: but why? Why do you believe that? And why should he choose you of all people,' she sobbed profusely again, 'when he knows—he must know, surely, if he is the Son of God—that you were complicit with a slatternly tribal girl in administering slow poison to your husband?'

Understandably, the priest did not quite grasp what she was saying. 'Oh yes, I do believe the poor Pastor was very ill towards the end.'

'Oh no, Father, you don't understand...I poisoned him!'

'Ah...' breathed Fr Roberto exasperatedly from the confessional box, 'are you sure you are not imagining things again, my child?'

'He was a monster, Father,' she said. 'He had been sleeping with this girl for months and years. Without my knowledge, of course, though later I began to suspect something of the sort.... And she was less than half his age!'

'Ah now, I'm very sure you are exaggerating, child,' said Fr Roberto. 'Ever since I came to Kerala, I have heard only good things about your deceased husband, the former Pastor. This is some sort of delusion that has gripped you, surely. Don't think about it...don't dwell on such things. They are just not true. Pray to our Lord for clarity.'

'Everyone has only a good word to say about the Pastor!' yelled Mary Agnes bristling with unexpected annoyance. 'Only that poor girl knows what she suffered at his hands. Finally, she decided to take her revenge.... And I being the monster he had always said I was fed homeopathic doses of poison to that same Pastor in his dinner, the same Pastor all the world chooses to believe was a saint!'

'Now, please be calm, Mary, my dear, please do stay calm,' said Fr Roberto, alarmed by the nascent hysteria in the voice that flared sharply at him through the apertures of the confessional. 'Everything will soon be alright....'

'Please, Father, please...it's years since anyone embraced me.... Please let me touch you.... Hold me, Fr Roberto...hold me....'

She tried to open the door of the confessional—but that only frightened the priest who held it fast from within.

Finally, ashamed of his inability to respond to her cry for help, he relented and opened the door a little. He put his hand out and squeezed her forearm gently. She seized his hand with both of hers, and pressed it to her lips.

'You are thinking too much, my child. Don't think so much. Don't think...let the love of Jesus enter your heart and do its work.'

Was it that—the love of Jesus—worked a transformation of her inner life?

Or articulating her own culpability (which the priest had refused to find credible) in her husband's death?

Or was it the heart Fr Roberto showed her in a moment of kindness when he allowed her to kiss his hand as though he were a pontiff?

Perhaps none of these: it could just as well have been an unusual addition to the support staff at the home who played a pivotal role in transfiguring her back to normality.

But the most significant symptom for her of recovery was that after months of barren sterility—ever since her brain surgery had taken place—she had once again begun to hear the voice of Jesus...in her solitary moments, in her dreams.

My dearly beloved daughter, as soon as you began to seriously disseminate my messages through the world, you became victim to Satan and his legion of devils. They danced around you in order to distract, torment and confuse you—harassed and interrupted at every second, they still try their utmost to prevent you from doing My Holy Will.

Soon, a time will come when the entire world see My Face again, illuminating the celestial expanses.

By then you can be sure that Satan will be a spent force, confined to an abyss under the earth for one thousand years.... Look after yourself, my dearest daughter, my Mary Agnes.

21

When I opened my eyes, I knew this was to be a special day.

For one thing, I sensed that I had managed somehow to crawl back into my own skin: I was Mary Agnes again, not a pathologically disturbed lunatic.

In full conversation with myself as in the old days, I thoroughly enjoyed my masala omelette and two slices of white bread—sampling this pristine fare as though for the first time in my life—steaming hot coffee, and an additional buttered bun too. I was brimming with confidence for the stroll I had planned to take in the Ashram's grounds.

∽

Stepping into the courtyard, I wandered onto the gravel pathway leading to the main garden.

At a considerable distance, and before anything else, my eyes lit upon a towering figure standing on a mound of floral exuberance at its centre: a man with a shock of frizzy hair tied at the back in a ponytail.

In all the weeks I had spent at the Ashram—could it be months already?—I had never set eyes on this man before.

Drawn magnetically, I sauntered in his direction: he returned my uninterrupted gaze with warmth and friendliness. Who is this stranger?

'That's Yesu....'

Responding to my noticeably intense gape, Sister Margarita prompted me in passing, 'Our new gardener. He has fabulous plans for the garden, he does, and Sister Clarissa has decided to give him a free hand.'

Sister Margarita strode briskly back to the main building; and I, as though captivated by a hypnotic spell, walked straight on to Yesu.

He greeted me as if we have known each other all our lives, his eyes full of kindness and affection.

'I am Yesuraj, the gardener. I know you, sister. You are Mary Agnes, aren't you?'

I stood there dumbfounded: that voice—something about it was unmistakably identical to the one I had heard so many times before—in my heart, in my mind, resounding in my dreams....

But even more than voice that manner: a soft, pure glow of love...his simple words enchanted me: I was convinced beyond a shadow of doubt that I stood in the presence of my Saviour.

He had come back after all.... Hallelujah! Jesus has been merciful. At last, he is back with us...but as a gardener?

'The kind sisters have been persuading me to redesign the garden, make it bloom and flourish again as it once did.'

I think of Mary Magdalene who entered the burial cave on the third morning only to find Jesus's sepulchre empty. Not far from her in the shadows stood the figure of the Risen Christ but she didn't recognize it was He...could this man perhaps be the local gardener, she wondered. Could he have moved the body of my Lord?

'Ah, yes, its glory was unsurpassed in those days. Everything I know about gardening I learned from my father. He created the most splendiferous gardens known to man—islands of unspoilt beauty and happiness—right here in Kerala.'

Now here I was, Mary Agnes, in full rapport with a simple, unsophisticated gardener.

'...sadly, all that is lost but can flourish again...here we have plenty of rain, sunshine, good soil. Light and nourishment are the bread of life, but tremendous amounts of pruning and clearing are needed...incorrigibly prickly thorns are everywhere... bramble, gorse...they must be uprooted, burned in a heap.'

....yet brimming with certainty that He is my Lord.

From the very bottom of my heart an intense current of rapture and wonderment electrified me.... Yes, Lord, as surely as the sun rises in the east, I know it is Thee.

Just then, as Yesu rambled on about how he would revivify the garden, another voice subsumed his: Pastor Pius's rich baritone reading to Mark and me from the Gospel of St Mathew. We were seated in our living room at Daeva Danam in the evening, we had just finished supper.

When he was come down from the mountains, great multitudes followed him.

And, behold, there came a leper and worshipped him, saying, Lord, if thou wilt, thou canst make me clean.

And Jesus put forth his hand and touched him, saying, I will; be thou clean. And immediately his leprosy was cleansed....

And Jesus went about all the cities and villages, teaching in their synagogues, and preaching the gospel of the kingdom, and healing every sickness and every disease among the people....

Yea, Lord! At last I know for sure I wasn't quite so mad when I heard Your Voice.

Your great authority had granted me divine audition.

Indisputably I wasn't dreaming or imagining things. Salvation is nigh, Praise the Lord…. Praise the Lord….

But my own anxieties may have imbued Jesus's words with perhaps more than was warranted, interpolating all the rancour and despair of my married life into his messages. Or was I merely trying to make a point, prove to the world how much better connected I was with the Lord than that lascivious husband of mine so inebriated on religious pretension?

No, the world won't end with a bang after all, perhaps not even with a whimper, surviving centuries more into the future…. The good Lord hadn't forsaken us yet: a penultimate totting up of invoices was underway even now, the final tally of the grand balance sheet still incomplete…. Thank You, O Lord, for all thy small and bountiful mercies…I'm in a better position now to understand your words of warning….

∽

Suddenly, I became aware of a great uproar on the grounds of the Ashram.

It wasn't the tumult of panic or calamity.

In an instant I recall: today is the day we have all been waiting for, Sister Clarissa Corda's boldest move thus far: a morning set aside by her for her inmates' first major outing, a sort of therapeutic picnic for the distracted—most of whom, I wouldn't be wrong in generalizing, appear quite definitely on the mend.

A motor launch has been booked to take all thirty-six of us (three opted out at the last minute due to indisposition) for a sort of trial outing on the backwaters of Alleppey.

At some pre-decided spot along the way, the sisters had promised we would stop for a special lunch in the open.

I turned and surveyed the scene—there they all were gathered in the courtyard, chaperoned by a handful of sisters. Jasper was there too, carrying a huge picnic basket and a large folded parasol under his arm. What arrested my attention a moment ago was only a general convulsion of merriment and laughter, everyone, including the sisters and Yesuraj beaming in its trail.

Soon we were seated in a boat, chugging along at a relaxed pace.

∽

I was in the rear behind the motor cabin, watching the gorgeous wake sparkle and spray into golden sunlight as we sliced through our very own Venice of the East.

Wooden seating rigged along the sides of the boat was fully occupied by the elderly and the infirm, while relatively young and healthier inmates had settled on the floor of the deck and gangway, areas lined with cane mats.

A moment of claustrophobia gripped me when I saw how many of us were cramped into so small a boat.

But none was in a mood to complain. Joyous as children setting off on a school picnic, everyone seemed to be thoroughly enjoying the novel experience.

Some broke into song, and it didn't take much persuasion for others to join in.

Gonzalo Nambiar was seated beside me on a bench.

Remarkably calmer than I had ever seen him before, he seemed to be enjoying the cool onrush of breeze and froth as we cruised along at a steady pace.

Now and then, I could hear him giggling softly to himself.

'Can I ask you a personal question, if you don't mind, Mr Gonzalo?'

I had to repeat this more than once before I was able to

catch his attention, 'How did you get a name like Gonzalo?'

When finally he understood me, the question set him off laughing with uncontrollable pleasure.

'Oh, dear, dear. Now let's see....how many years ago it was, such an old story. You see, my real name is forgettable, completely run-of-the-mill—Ganesh Nambiar...yes, that's me. In the old days everyone called me "Goncase" Nambiar...that made me terribly dejected. So one day I thought, why not invent a more respectable name? Gonzalo? Like a Spanish feudal lord? And not so terribly different at that from Ganesh or Goncase, wouldn't you say?'

I joined in his laughter, and ventured to ask him yet another question:

'And what is it makes you laugh quietly to yourself from time to time?'

'Those bubbles...don't you see them? Those delicious bubbles,' he said, indicating the receding wake frothing behind us. 'Today I feel happier than I've been in a very long time....'

Practically submerged under the picnickers' raucous warbling, our conversation remained perfunctory, yet gratifying to both of us.

I looked around and casually surveyed smiling faces on the boat; amazingly, for the first time since we started off from the Ashram jetty, I noticed that Yesuraj: the gardener had come along too!

I was delighted. Had I spotted him earlier I would surely have grabbed a seat closer to him. I stood up abruptly and started moving in his direction through the crush of passengers, intent on making it to the other end of the boat—people protested: no, no room—hang on, watch out, ouch!—I shuffled and inched past persons occupying the deck area avoiding hands, knobbly knees, fragile digits…and once again that sense of alarm: this boat is much too small for so many of us!

All manner of disorder obstructed my path (a large picnic basket for one, an even larger metal tiffin box, various personal carry-bags, satchels, handbags, an assortment of rubber slippers, a rusted and dangerous-looking anchor whose curving tip protruded from beneath a bench and, most of all, well, so many—people); I inconvenienced them I know, but was much too exhilarated to care.

Thinking that it would be simpler to walk along the narrow side-guard of the launch, I threw caution to the winds and climbed onto the steel rail running along the boat's hull. Balancing by holding onto the overhead canopy while walking the rod affixed to the side of the boat—an acrobatic feat doubtless worthy of Flying Koel in his heyday—I steadily proceeded towards where Yesu was sitting; pulled, as it were by a force outside my control.

Oh dear, oh dear, before I had crossed no more than three or four feet—oh no: aaiiee!

Unexpectedly, and with a sudden jerk the boat had stalled: I slipped, lost my foothold, fingers not strong enough to hold on to the overhead canvas—and splash! In an instant I was in the river, fully drenched.

'Yesu!' I screamed, swallowing a great deal of murky water. 'Save me!'

'I can't swim!' Yesuraj shouted back.

There was water everywhere, in my eyes, ears, nose, all around me. I was afraid the launch would start puttering again and leave me floundering in its discharge; but in the very next instant there was a loud explosion, and the motor cabin was engulfed in smoke.

The boat was now at a total standstill, dead. What treachery is this? A bomb?

Chaos, screams of panic, a few sober voices of authority urging calm and restraint...all this I heard from the water. Later, I was told there were a few licks of flame as well, quickly doused by the attendant using his bottle of drinking water.

Luckily, what had occurred was only a relatively minor mishap caused by the build-up of volatile gases in the engine of the outboard motor—no explosive or evil terrorist design—the engine just hadn't been opened and aired in days as it should have prior to our setting off on this excursion.

All this, as I said, I learnt later.

And myself, in the water, I was not panicking any more. Although I can't swim, I had remembered I know how to stay afloat.

When the motor exploded, fortunately we weren't far from a riverbank, and in fairly shallow waters.

The sisters showed remarkable calm and efficiency, other passengers were inspired to emulate their composure.

Thankfully, there were no casualties except those self-inflicted by shock and alarm: one old woman passed out for quite a while before she came to again, another's hands kept trembling unstoppably until hugged and caressed by her neighbour; the motor attendant was the only one in some pain having received burn injuries on his forearm and face; presently, these too were salved by ointment from the boat's first aid kit.

After wading through, and disentangling myself from, dense expanses of water hyacinth I had to paddle but a short distance through murky water before clambering onto solid ground.

Thick-leafed thorny vegetation, baby coconut shoots and fronds were profusely entangled in nameless undergrowth on a bank of what may possibly have been a tributary of the Achankovil River—this name I had heard bandied about knowledgeably by picnickers several times since we set out from the Ashram.

First to have made it to shore, I was soon joined there by Sister Benito, most athletic of the nuns.

Two attendants of the stranded, now silent motor-launch—one a mere boy—assisted the sisters in getting passengers off the boat and encouraging them to wade to terra firma. Only a few of the very old or very rattled had to be led by hand all the way along the slippery, squelchy riverbed towards where Sister Benito and I stretched out and pulled them in.

As might be expected, everyone was entirely soaked: the sisters' habits had lost their starch and some of their forbidding grace; a few old persons were captive to paroxysms of sneezing; but it being a hot day and, with willingness to accept the disaster as unavoidable—none of us much the worse for it—soon we were stretched out in exhaustion on the tall grass and fern catching our breath, allowing the sun to dry our clothes and dank spirits.

As for myself, I was under a dreadful pall of gloom, terribly depressed and disappointed.

With myself, to be sure, no one else.... It took me a while to figure out why.

And finally I understand: here was one emotional or psychological habit I hadn't outgrown in decades!

In infancy and childhood it was Dad I had thought the world of. For me, he could do no wrong.

Later, as a young woman, although perhaps only for a while, it was Amma Rosalie who wore the nimbus of glorification: my entirely inarticulate hurt and anger identifying with what I saw as her marital desertion.

But quite soon after, mindless devotion transferred itself onto my husband, the late Pastor Pius Philipose.

And now, as elderly widow possibly of unsound mind, I had

once again been gripped by that old habit—of pinning every ounce of hope and love and belief on one individual: a simple gardener called Yesu, convinced that he was indeed resurgent Christ who had appeared in the world again in accordance with scriptural prediction.

That, in this final hour—when it is time for the seventh trumpet to blast the death knell of a world overrun by the wicked and ungodly—Jesus had, as foretold, made His triumphant Second Coming.

As Yesu? A simple gardener?

Well, why not? Give it a moment's thought and you'll see there's nothing so preposterous about the idea....

Ah, Mary Agnes...aren't we being disingenuous again? How well you had analysed the invalidity of your remarkable hypothesis only a few moments ago! Or don't you remember, Mary, for heaven's sake?

Let alone not being able to walk on water, this Yesu can't even swim.

And what's more as further you probed your soul's wild and random clamouring...until just a while ago your mind was toying with the promise of witnessing even more extraordinary miracles—from Yesu!

It's true. I won't deny it.

Old Jasper, while climbing out of the dysfunctional motor launch tried to carry more articles of luggage than he could possibly handle; with the result that he fell clumsily in the water. In panic, he had released his grip on the picnic basket's cane handle and, our entire lunch, painstakingly packed by the Ashram's kitchen staff to feed forty or fifty of us, sank swiftly to opaque riverine depths like a stone.

But in that very instant a jubilant beam of hope had flashed brilliantly at my heart: never mind, Mary Agnes, what's the big deal about a lunch basket? Yesu's with us, isn't he?

Now, lying in the damp grass among rows of other aged and absent-minded persons I dissected what it was had enthralled me so a moment ago—not just foolish possibility, my mind had already transformed the yearning for prodigious marvels into actual event—soon, I was convinced, we would witness another exponential multiplication of two fishes and five loaves—surely Yesu would materialize some food from somewhere—then augment it manifold to satiate the appetite of our waterlogged and relatively small party—as when the disciples had distributed portions of fish and loaves to Jesus's attentive but famished audience of five-thousand strong—sackfuls left over, even after everyone ate their fill.

A sumptuous feast, I was certain we were in for. And Yesu, the gardener, would manifest it any moment.

But when it was late afternoon, light waning and many of us experiencing mild hunger pangs as we waited in chary anticipation for the chugging of our replacement motorboat to be heard, I understood just how gullible one can be in matters of faith—or at least I could be—just how thin the dividing line between sanity and madness is when one decides to embrace conviction.

Faith can move mountains, yes, many do believe this. Which makes it reasonable, or even desirable, never to lose faith in the prospect of miracles: in the naked expectation that one's flimsiest fantasy will somehow transfigure into rock-solid reality.

But the greater truth perhaps is that mere faith never displaced nor so much as stirred a single pebble in the entire geography of the earth.

In retrospect though, I must admit I may have been

completely wrong to latch on to so facile and cynical a conclusion: for what happened when we went to bed that night, and the following morning, was little short of miraculous.

I can't think of any other word.

∽

That night an angel came to me in a dream.

I knew he was the Angel Gabriel, glowing and radiant with light. His first concern of course was to soothe my alarm at his blinding refulgence.

And then when he spoke, his words sounded reassuring and vaguely familiar:

Hail Mary Agnes, do not be afraid. Thou art highly favoured, the Lord is with thee: blessed art thou among women.... Fear not, Mary, for thou hast found favour with God...behold, thou shalt conceive in thy womb, and bring forth a son, and his name shall be—

Ah, I never did find out. For in that very moment my sleep was disturbed by a loud bird cry, possibly an owl's hooting, momentary disturbance that simply bleeped out the angel's words, and made me miss hearing my son's name.

Swiftly, and deliberately, I dived back into deeper sleep with a powerful longing to seat myself once again at the feet of the archangel and drink in the music of that name.

But this time I slept too deep and dreamlessly.

When I woke up again, it was hard daylight. I was feeling completely refreshed. Vaguely, I recalled our hectic adventures of the previous day.

It was hard daylight and Parvati appeared with a cup of coffee for me, a faint, conspiratorial smile flickering on her lips as she announced I had a visitor.

No! Hang on. What's this?

Can't be…Parvati? I am still here in my dorm at the Ashram for the mentally afflicted! Nowhere near Daeva Danam, please!

I rubbed my eyes and opened them once again.

This time I focussed more clearly. It was only Sister Pietra, a young novitiate who had joined the order very recently… although she *had* brought me a cup of coffee!

That itself was most unusual. In the normal course of things there is never any room service here, we are expected to troop down to the cafeteria for breakfast.

'Sister Clarissa wants you to come to her office after you have freshened up. There's someone waiting there to meet you.'

I nearly scalded my tongue on the hot coffee, mind agog with guessing who it could possibly be. I slipped out of my nightclothes, made myself decent and headed straight for Sister Clarissa's office.

I was amazed, dumbstruck, delighted: my visitor was none other than my only son, Mark.

Seeing him though after what may have been close to twenty years, I didn't find myself gasping with surprise. Could my dream of the previous night have prepared me for his unexpected advent?

'Mark…!'

We embraced.

'Oh, Mark, after all these years? Where have you been? Tell me everything…I missed you, Mark, I've missed you….'

'We'll have plenty of time to talk, Mama,' he said.

'Have you come to take me home?' I asked.

Sister Clarissa smiled when she heard that, and shook her head.

'Not as yet, Mary Agnes,' she said, 'You still have to get completely well first, before I let you go home…. And you will too, soon. I'm sure…'

Then, excusing herself for a few minutes, Sister Clarissa left Mark and me alone in her office. We talked.

'Do you remember my school friend, Nelson?' Mark asked me.

'Nelson?'

'Nelson Kuruvilla.... Three years my senior actually but I was always drawn to him. A generous and intelligent person even at that age when most of us behaved like real devils.

'He allowed me to live at his place in Delhi when I left home.

'Off and on, I stayed with him for several years. And even later, when he moved almost permanently to Andhra Pradesh, he continued to let me live there....

'Essentially he was a trade union activist. At the time I speak of he was very involved with the struggle asbestos mining workers were waging at a small town in Andhra called Kadapa....

'I learned so much from him, from his political understanding of the world, how corrupt and decayed bourgeois society can be, how sick and unhealthy all those institutions we are expected to revere and swear by.... Including the family, Mama, yes, including the nuclear family.

'No, I couldn't possibly have continued to live with you and Appa. When I ran away I had no choice, it was my only road to survival.... I'm sorry if I made you worry.'

'Never mind, Mark...' I said, softly. 'It's all over now....'

'And when Appa died I felt such horrible loss.... All the things I would have liked to discuss with him, but never got down to...I felt so cheated....'

'Yes, dear, your Appa left early,' I commiserated. 'What to do? You should have come home to me then.'

'I had only just started at a full-time office job. My bosses weren't prepared to give me leave. Anyway I didn't continue much longer there and soon went back to journalism—my freelancing.'

I was listening with rapt attention. I waited anxiously as if anticipating something more dreadful was about to be revealed.

'About six years ago Nelson asked me if I'd like to come visit him in Kadapa, and maybe do a piece on the striking miners. By now he was himself based there, and the asbestos miners' strike had entered its fifteenth month. Two miners had only just died of asbestosis. Workers were agitating, among other things, for the company to pay their health insurance premiums.

'Late one night as we were walking back to Nelson's lodge in Kadapa we were stopped by a police jeep.... The cops picked up Nelson for being what they called a troublemaker and for disturbing the peace. They didn't have a warrant for him, of course, but said they wanted him to come along for questioning.

'I tried to get into the jeep with him but they pushed me out and drove away.... I never saw Nelson again. Three days later, his body was found in the woods off the Tirumala hills, with a single bullet in the back of his head. This time the cops called me to the morgue, ostensibly for identification. But once that was done, they arrested me.

'Whose interests were the cops protecting? No one knows, the newspapers only reported the "mysterious death of a dreaded Naxalite", speculating about possible internecine Maoist rivalry.

'I was the only witness to his kidnapping, so I can understand why they arrested me as well, charging me with aiding and abetting a Naxalite, but to that they added a dozen cases even more fictional....

'In Bengaluru Central Jail I was an undertrial for six years. I had to cope with many hardships, but only for a surprisingly short time. Other prisoners I met had been rotting in jail for much, much longer. I feared too that I would never come out alive again, that I'd never see you again, or get a chance to explain to you where I'd been. But someone who knew Nelson from his days in PUCL found a lawyer for me and expedited my case: finally all charges against me were summarily dismissed by a High Court judge in the course of the last four months.... I was very lucky.... Except for one more case. Which is slated to come up next month.... I discovered after a phone call to your caretaker at Daeva Danam where you were. The judge allowed me parole to be able to come and visit you. But I have to report back to my jailer next week.'

'But why didn't you get in touch with me earlier? I might have been able to help you—'

'Frankly, I didn't think so, Mama. And more than that, I didn't want to give you any further reason for worry than I already had....'

Sister Corda came back into her office just then. We got up to take our leave. She shook hands with both of us.

Mark thanked her profusely for the time his mother had spent at the Ashram.

'You can stay on for lunch with your mother. We have simple fare at the cafeteria, but it's edible.'

As we walked away to spend the morning in the lounge area, I noticed for the first time that my son was limping. He appeared to have developed a slight limp in his right leg. I was grateful to the Lord that my son had been spared what could possibly have been much worse by way of suffering. It was as if, I mused, Mark had been raised like Lazarus from the dead.

∽

'Poor Dad,' said Mark to me once we were seated beside each other on one of the long sofas in the lounge area. 'I didn't get a chance to explain my long absence to him.'

'There were days when he remembered you,' I said, 'missed you…but always so busy he was with his parish work. But I'm sure he understands, wherever he is now….'

'One of the things I would have liked to ask him—if he were still around…why does death invariably come to us as such a surprise?'

'For all of us death is inevitable, Mark, we know that. And your father had been ailing for months.'

'And yet when it ambushes us it evokes the wildest surprise and disbelief? That strange coldness of death's touch…I felt it for the first time when I laid my hands on Kuruvilla's dead body.'

'As though,' I added, elaborating on Mark's line of thought, 'it were the very last thing in the world one could possibly expect. Even though in fact it is the only thing that's certain to happen to each one of us from the day of our birth!'

'Exactly. Maybe this feeling of strangeness arises because of a transubstantiation of sorts?'

'What do you mean?'

'When spirit is voided from matter an entirely different substance is created. The corpse hasn't the remotest connection with the living being it once was.'

'Maybe you're right,' I said. 'It must be something like that. But why are we thinking these morbid thoughts, Mark?'

'Morbid? No, these questions are central to life, I believe….'

After that exchange, both of us sat there in silence for a while. Soon, it was almost time for an early lunch at the cafeteria.

'What will you do now, Mark?'

'On Tuesday morning, I must report back to Bengaluru Jail. In the weeks to follow, with some luck, the last of my cases will come up for hearing at the High Court. And, with more luck, that too should be dismissed like the rest of them. But, while I still have two free days, I think I will spend them at Daeva Danam.'

'That's what I was just going to suggest,' I said. 'You should. It's your farm now.'

'I will, sure I will…. It will be a very relaxing two days,' said Mark.

'I will be there with you in spirit…thinking of you always, my son.'

∽

When he got back to Daeva Danam a few hours later, Peter and Parvati welcomed Mark home.

It was already evening. For a long while, Mark continued to stroll in the garden amidst the trees, the meandering overgrown pathways.

And though Parvati complained that the coffee she had made for him had gone cold—and finally brought it out on a tray after re-heating it—he couldn't bring himself to go indoors or stop marvelling at the russet and amber of his mother's autumnal spice garden, through whose vines, shrubs and slender boles fresh and gusty breezes were blowing uninterruptedly.

How do I know?

I was there.

Acknowledgements

I am grateful to Milburn Cherian, first of all, for giving me a seed of an idea that grew into a novel.

To David and Dixie for allowing Jill and me to hitch a ride from Kodaikanal to Cochin, thus enabling our first-ever visit to Kerala to begin on so pleasant a note.

To Lathika George for facilitating our equally pleasant homestay with Kurien and Molly George in Anakkal, as also for being a constant information resource on Malayali culture and language. To Roy Kallarakkal, and Mark Antrobus for initiating our first glimpses into the world of cardamom-growing. To George Abraham and family of Koottikal for their hospitality, and also to Kurien Kubikany and his daughter-in-law, Sheryl, many thanks.

To the late A. K. Ramanujan with whom I had the privilege of working as a young playwright during a translation project in Mumbai: for a version of the Kurumba folk tale which appears in his collection *Folk Tales of India*.

And last but not least, to Jayshree Kumar for her support and friendship.